"It's brilliant. And the greatest thing in it is the most important thing in any great novel: the sentences."

—**Henry Bean**, *Internal Affairs*, *The Believer*

"An amped-up, absurdist version of *The Player*. Demonstrating a giddy sense of boundless energy, Novak skewers everything about the biz with a machine-gun fusillade on every page."

—**Ben Sitzer**, CAA

"Opening any page and fastening onto a sentence is like touching a live wire. Novak's prose, alive with concentrated energy, casually spinning off epigrams, announces a new voice and a large talent."

—**Brian O'Doherty**, *The Deposition of Father McGreevey*, short-listed for the 2000 Booker Prize

12.14.2010

The NON-PRO

CAT–

A good egg...

The NON-PRO

Adam Novak

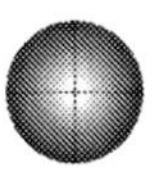

Salvo Press
Portland, Oregon

This is a work of fiction. All characters and events portrayed in this novel are fictitious and not intended to represent real people or places.

THE NON-PRO

Salvo Press, LLC
P.O. Box 7396
Beaverton, OR 97007

www.salvopress.com

Visit the author online at www.thenonpro.com
Cover Photo by Lauren Mann

Library of Congress Control Number: 2007940916

ISBN: 1-930486-75-8
9781930486751

Printed in U.S.A.
First Edition

For Bob Maners and John Ptak
—who got me in

LOS ANGELES TIMES

JERRY MAKOS, 28, HOLLYWOOD AGENT SUSPECTED VICTIM OF FOUL PLAY

LOS ANGELES—Police are investigating the apparent homicide of Jerry Makos, one of Hollywood's "Top 100 People You Need to Know." A spokesperson declined to say how he died. There have been no arrests or charges in the case.

Makos, a rising agent within the powerhouse talent agency Omniscience, was best known for championing the script for the film "Faith Don't Leave," which achieved blockbuster status.

Omniscience's world-wide head of motion pictures Lester Barnes said, "Jerry was one of the good eggs; I'm going to miss him terribly, as will, I know, Omniscience and all of our clients."

Makos is survived by a brother.

Before he was murdered, I discovered my brother had arrived in the movie business. Jerry and I were having dinner at some club called the Mink Slide where he was pitching a script he'd read about aliens mistaken for Catholic priests by these Valley girls, something like that, how they all fall in love, but not before the aliens report back to their evil ruler Mordor or some Hjortsberg nonsense that the planet isn't worth destroying—

"Riddle me this, my brother: why is the Vatican in Rome? Why isn't it in Jerusalem, where Jesus lived and died? I'll tell you: The Bible was written by the Romans after they crucified this smiling Jew named Jesus who had a big mouth and wouldn't stop spilling it about love thy neighbor and turn thy cheek! The Romans were smart: they heard the pitch first and they jumped on it! Turned it into a 2000 year old franchise! I hope they promoted the centurion who had the bright idea to whack Jesus, steal his script, order a page one rewrite, promise the world an afterlife, install a pope of production who's totally beholden to the money guys, inflict mass murder on the millions of people who gave it a bad review and call it the 'Crusades.' I mean, talk about vertical integration!"

"I never heard the Vatican pitched that way," said this unshaven guy wearing a Welcome Back Kotter T-shirt with lime green pants, eating alone at a table next to ours. "Are you in the Industry?"

"What industry?" asked Jerry.

I volunteered that my brother worked at an agency called Omniscience.

"You're at Omniscience? I bet you know my friend Jerry Makos, he's an icon over there," said Lone Eater.

"You know Jerry Makos?" asked my brother.

"He's my buddy! Hey, I didn't catch your name," said Lone Eater.

"You sure we haven't met?" said Jerry.

"I don't think so," said Lone Eater.

"I'm Jerry Makos."

Yeah, my brother had made it. Who gets name-dropped to their face?

I told that story as part of my eulogy in the herb garden of Les Deux, a shrubbery-lined restaurant off Sunset Boulevard behind a filthy street where homeless panhandlers share the sidewalk with Scientology recruiters when this 30-something brunette comes up to me, Madras in one hand, as if she were clubbing instead of mourning at Jerry's "celebration of life" service.

"I liked what you said about your brother," says Madras.

"They call me Josh," I say.

"Stefani Dupin."

"So, how well did you know my brother?"

"There was this bachelorette party at The Key Club in Hermosa. We were all drunk as shit. My girlfriends dared me to take a guy home with me. It had been a while."

"What's a while?"

"God, I don't know, a week, at least," she says.

No more Diet Cokes for me. I order what she's having. A bad idea, I know, but I need to get numb, fast.

"So, anyways, I go over to your brother and we start talking. He does this adorable trick with a dollar bill that cracks me up and I'm thinking, OK, if this guy makes me laugh again we are definitely going back to my place."

I raise the pink drink to my lips, thinking, "Jerry's dead.

Jerry's dead. Here's to you, bro—"

"My girlfriends dragged us to the dance floor and Jerry cracked me up again so I kissed him and he started calling me 'unprofessional.' I was so drunk I didn't quite catch his drift," she laughs.

I try to concentrate on her mindless story to keep myself from screaming.

"We left together and it ended up being really great. The next morning your brother started telling me about this premiere he went to all by his lonesome. Wanted to know if I knew so and so? And I go 'Who?' Then he asked me, what's my rate for premieres?"

It takes me a second. "He thought you were a pro."

"Eggs-actly. He thought this agent named Arthur paid me to fuck his brains out. I said, 'I only did you because my girlfriends dared me to.'"

The sky threatens to go black.

"I bet you most of the people here didn't even know Jerry." I glance around at the anonymous dark suits dotting the garden.

"Maybe they're here for the contacts," her eyes trail mine across the scene.

"Maybe they're here to make sure he's dead."

"Well, I'm here to find the guy who did it," she meets my gaze, eyes narrowing. "Did Jerry ever tell you about someone, a competitor, a studio executive who he particularly hated?"

"You sound like a detective in a movie," I joke.

Detective Stefani Dupin hands me her LAPD business card with a pager number, cell phone, and e-mail address—

"Now you know how to reach me, just call 911."

•

Spellbound by the leafy, roof-littered Beachwood canyon landscape, I can see the Hollywood sign from the rustic deck of Jerry's house in the hills. I find a heavy hitting bag chained to a makeshift boxing area, a speed bag, and Jerry's blue, 16 oz boxing gloves, carelessly left outside. Scrawled on the gloves, a name: TERRONDUS. Jerry's ranch-style shed has one bedroom, one bathroom (one shower, no tub, pink tiles), a dining room and kitchen surrounded by a panoramic floor-to-ceiling window. I pull a light bulb string in his garage to reveal a tribe of rolled up movie posters. I slide off a rubber band, roll open Second Coming, a teen comedy about this high school cheerleader who turns out to be the Anti-Christ. Flash of a blade cutting Jerry's throat. Another straight-to-video called The Mighty Mite, about the war between a flea named Frankie and the St. Bernard from the Beethoven movies who looked like he'd seen better days. Flash of Jerry gagging on hot thick carotid juice. Then there was Ajax, an unbelievably cheesy abominable snowman-terrorizing-snowboarders affair. I'm wondering what Jerry had to do with these movies until I recognize our mother's ex-boyfriend listed as an executive producer. The only thing Jerry and I had in common was a profound disgust for this dry-cleaning warlord we called the Bug, who reinvented himself as a movie producer after investing in some piece of trash about a saber tooth tiger run amok. Of course we blamed him after Mom dropped dead on the treadmill he had bought her so she could get in shape to re-ignite his interest in her as a depository to waste his sick seed.

Going through Jerry's mail, I find health mags promoting ripped abs, credit card bills, and a pink envelope sealed with a ruby red lipstick kiss to a party celebrating the anniversary of CyberWhore.com (secret password:

Gianni Roastbeef). I read a high-lighted Daily Variety article about Jerry's boss announcing TEN-PERCENTER GETS 0%:

"Omniscience worldwide head of motion pictures Lester Barnes officially exited the agency on Thursday after he admitted lying about rumors of his departure. In a recent staff meeting, unidentified sources say, Mr. Barnes got emotional with his colleagues and suggested that everyone in the company tune in to his channel, instead of letting the street disrupt their house with their vicious lies. Lester Barnes had, in fact, been in final negotiations with a fizzling, fiscally extravagant movie studio, holding secret meetings in strip clubs and hotel suites under code names when someone inside the agency ruined the negotiations by exposing Mr. Barnes and his clandestine affair. Also rumored was a hit list of Omniscience employees thought to be open to joining him at the top of the studio."

I make myself a triple Absolut Mandrin with a lot of ice in a heavy Tiffany tumbler and pace the house like one of those pathetic polar bears I saw at the Los Angeles Zoo, ready to call the airlines, ready to leave L.A. when the phone rings—

"I have Lester Barnes calling from the car," announces an assistant with a Southern accent.

"Jessica, stay on the line with me, do not get off the phone! Josh, I'm dealing with a new assistant who doesn't know her twat from her elbow. Let's not talk while she's on the line. I can tell you what a cunt she is later. Are you free tonight? I'd like to meet you."

"I didn't see you at the memorial service," I say.

"Again, the assistant. Bitch had me scheduled for a screening at Columbia. Hold on—Crazy asshole!"

Lester leans on his horn for a good ten seconds.

"Sorry, some guy in a Navigator just cut me off. I'm on

Ventura," he says.

I don't believe this guy. He comes through over the phone like a cartoon character, word balloons popping out of his Range Rover window.

"Can't we discuss Jerry right now? I'm not staying here much longer," I say.

"We can't talk right now. We're not on a secure line. Jessica's probably playing Tetris. Right, Jessica? I'm crossing Lankershim."

"Mr. Barnes. What am I, OnStar?"

"Call me Lester. How about tonight? Jessica, come back on the line—"

"All right, where?"

"Hold on, I lost Jessica, let me think! I got it! Meet me at the top of the Hotel Angelino by the 405!"

I don't know which is more startling, Lester's choice of rendezvous, or my absurd decision to take a meeting with the Boogeyman.

Like most aging icons in the city, the Hotel Angelino has had some work done. The rooftop bar hostess leads me to a table by the window overlooking the 405 freeway. There I find a morbidly obese man in a black Prada suit talking to himself. It takes me a second to realize he's actually on a call. Lester Barnes ends the conversation, yanks his earpiece, and offers me a firm, welcoming left handshake—

"Are you going to eat that?" I ask, pointing to the Blackberry deposited on his plate.

"Christ, you look just like Jerry," says Lester.

"I should. I'm his brother."

"Jerry never mentioned you were a pro. Still stringing rackets at Palmetto Dunes?"

"How'd you—"

"1998 runner-up to Alex Corretja, Scottsdale Classic, blew your knee out against Paradorn Srichapan in the second round of the Pacific Life Open, followed by retirement, rehab and an arrest for brawling in the streets of Stockholm!"

"You googled me. What is this, a date?"

Rastafarian waitress arrives to take our order.

"Josh, get whatever harpoons your whale."

"Vodka cran sounds good to me. Do you have Absolut Mandrin?"

"Mandrin? Is that the bomb? I'll have the same," says Lester.

Waitress tells us she'll be right back.

"You see the ass on that whore?" sneers Lester.

"I missed it," I say.

"They're all crazy cunts out here, Josh. Right now I'm fucking this deranged woman named Liza. You know how I met her? Oh God, this is so fucked up, I can't believe I'm—anyways, I spot this babe Liza sucking margaritas at El Carmen. I tell her I've got Oxy-Contin, twenty minutes later I'm pounding her like a piece of veal."

"I'm calling the ASPCA," I say.

"We should play sometime. I have a grass court at my house, you know. If you're thinking of selling Jerry's house, use my broker Stella at Fred Sands, she just had vaginal rejuvenation surgery. Sculpted lips, daddy stitch, her walls completely re-done Art Deco," says Lester.

"You two must be very close," I say.

"Tell me Josh, you going back or are you going to chance it out here?"

"I'm not leaving till they catch the guy who did it."

"No justice, no peace. I'm throwing a little Emmy party this weekend. Bring that Baretta who interrogated me, she was smoking hot!"

Rastafarian waitress reappears with our drinks.

"Jerry, put your wallet away. Whoever talks the most, pays—"

"I'm Josh. You just called me Jerry."

"Goddamn, I'm sorry," says Lester.

"No worries. I'll take Stella's number, she sounds cool."

"She's a fruitcake. Did I tell you I'm banging this woman named Liza who's deranged? I get these suicidal calls from her, how life is meaningless since her TV show got cancelled. I leave work to console this bitch at her apartment. I pay for her TiVo and all she does is threaten to kill herself five times a day like a Muslim!"

"Run Lester run!"

"Don't be cruel, Josh. She dumped her boyfriend after

she scored the pilot, then drove away all her friends with her cocaine habit. Now she's obsessed with Marilyn Monroe's abortionist. I tried to get her to have her tubes tied, but she told me no way anybody's going to touch Madame Ovary's tubes!"

"May I be frank with you?"

"Only if I can be Lester," he says. "Do you need money?"

"No, that's not—was my brother going to jump?"

"Jerry was not suicidal," says Lester.

"Was he on your list?"

"Do I look like Oscar Schindler? Anybody who has to write down a list of his enemies has too many enemies. I keep them all up here in my head," says Lester.

"Was Jerry one of the agents you were going to take with you to the studio?"

"Stop reading the trades," he says.

"What are you going to do now that you've left Omniscience?"

"I'm going to Disneyland!"

Driving back to Beachwood on Canyon Drive, I slow past a silver Porsche Boxster wrapped around a tree. The car is totaled, so is the driver, who comes up to my window like a wraith—

"Dude! I need to use your car! It's an emergency!"

I instantly recognize the actor, whose name escapes me, as the star of Caesar High, a popular tits & zits series set in and around Ancient Rome.

"You want me to take you to a hospital?"

"Do I look like I need to go to Cedars? We gotta go! Come on, it's almost closing time," says the Actor, sliding across the front hood of my car.

"What about your Porsche?"

"It's a loaner! Let's hit the Slide," he says, opening the passenger door.

"The what?"

"The Mink Slide," he says into my ear.

"In Silver Lake?"

"You know it, let's go!"

Actor starts telling me about this one-act play he's thinking of writing for himself so he can be "taken more seriously." He calls it The Martini Shot, about this "woman who's a lawyer" sitting in the bar at the Beverly Wilshire Hotel rolling calls with her assistant, trying to "anesthetize herself after a quickie" she just had with a client who still hasn't left his wife for her, not yet, when she realizes the gentleman sitting next to her is a major movie star:

"What are you drinking?" asks the lawyer.

"Poison," says the major movie star.

"What kind?" asks the lawyer.

"The kind that kills," says the major movie star.

"I didn't know there was any other kind," says the lawyer.

"There's people," says the major movie star.

"The slow-acting kind," says the lawyer.

"I have a need for a will, do you have a way?"

"I'm off-duty right now, but here's my card. Call me Monday," she says.

"I won't be around Monday," he says.

"Try," she says.

Actor tells me how the lawyer and the star get sloppy drunk, go upstairs where her client only hours ago fucked her from behind in the room she paid for on the company dime. The lawyer writes down his will on hotel stationary, persuades the suicidal star to improv a scene from her life where he tells her how much he adores her, how he's just told his wife he wants a divorce. Major movie star makes love to her, realizes he just gave the performance of his life. He no longer wants to kill himself, so he crumples up the will and finds his way to the door. Lawyer feels exactly the way she did before: fucked and alone. She ends up jumping off the hotel balcony to her death. Actor tells me his plan is to "workshop it" as a play, then "do it as a short," make it as "an indie" and get a "big domestic sale" at Sundance. I wait for subtitles, but they never appear.

Entering this club feels exactly like when Captain Kirk and his crew endure the transporter room to enter another world. Every molecule scrambles in order to disappear and re-assemble somewhere else. I walk in surrounded by the warmth of dark crimson walls and a mellow vibe that makes me want to close my eyes and breathe it all in. Turning past the regatta of cosmos, gimlets, 7&7s, and Red Bull martinis, I realize the Mink Slide isn't very big at all. But when I see where the drinks are poured the place suddenly becomes huge in my mind. Mirrors stretch across the ceiling and walls: this place has a past. My eyes slide down a gleaming ceiling-to-floor brass pole in the middle of a 360° cherry wood bar. Some chick in a black halter top screams Siobhan! Over here! Siobhan! The bartender slinks over to the shrieking girl, but I can't see Siobhan's face yet because it's four rows deep at the bar. I hear the same chick again with the Siobhan! Over here! I push into the crowd and come face to face with the bartender, fake eyelashes, fake everything, her battle-hardened features back-lit with the gleaming bottles. Telepathically, Siobhan asks: Are you the Messiah? Scotch and soda? Amstel Light?

"Stoli-Vanilla, no, make it a Mandrin and—"

Siobhan shovels ice into a sweaty highball and makes my drink while taking orders from a bunch of fools. Her almond eyes widen with expectancy, and…?

"Mandrin, rocks. That's it," I say.

The bartender simultaneously pours a row of kamikazes, slaps the taps, blows off the head, and takes an impulsive, greedy gulp of pale ale under a spigot. She comes back with my drink. I respond telepathically: Do you know who I am? Do I matter to you at all? Are you someone's reason to live?

"No charge, Jerry," says the bartender.

I start to tell her I am not my brother; that Jerry is dead, but Siobhan exits my view so she can settle tabs and collect signatures. When she holds the pole in the center of her bar for support and leans forward, breasts spilling out, to collect dollar bills, she looks just like a proud stripper. I check my reflection in the mirror behind the bottles and see an ancient piano player, white hair, playing a medley from "Cheers," the theme from "SWAT," and "The Greatest American Hero," and ending with "Friends" when this raven haired smoker startles me—

"Guy at the piano used to be a prodigy. If you believe what they say," Raven says.

"Who's they?"

"Owners found him eating out of their dumpsters and instead of calling the police hired him to sweep the outside area. That piano was just for show until he sat down and played Rachmanoff, some savant shit like that, you know?"

I notice a lime floating at the bottom of her bottle and offer to buy her another Pacifico. We introduce ourselves: Vivian, Josh. Josh, Vivian.

"What are we toasting?"

"To collecting unemployment again!" says Vivian, rattling the soggy lime.

"You got fired, too?"

As if being unemployable is a badge. When I ask Vivian what happened, she tells me her temp agency busted her for lying about her typing skills.

"What's your sad story, Josh?"

I think about unleashing the tale of my brother's murder, but that's a buzz killer so I decide to tell her a Jerry story as if it happened to me—

"You know who Gary Oldman is, right?"

Vivian nods, of course.

"Well, I work with his agent Arty Livingstone," I say.

"Arty calls from the Cannes Film Festival, says he needs me to find Gary Oldman and put him on a plane to London for a meeting with a director. I tell Arty, 'Don't worry. I'll call you from the car at LAX after I've dropped Gary off.' Arty goes to sleep at his hotel in Cannes. I drive around the city calling Gary's fucking useless personal assistants."

"Fucking useless," Vivian laughs.

I smile and give her thoughtful eye contact so she won't think I'm a jerk who's only interested when the lights are on and her clothes are off.

"This girl I know tells me Gary kick-boxes at Crunch in the afternoon. He's not there. I drive to my friend's house, get the digits to a DJ who sold Gary some incense, he tells me Gary went out to surf by Neptune's Net, right by the Ventura county line—ever had a squid burger?"

Vivian shakes her head.

"I'll take you," I say. "So I drive all the way to Neptune's Net, no Gary. I run out into the water and start asking these guys if they know Gary Oldman, and have they seen him? Finally, some girl in the curl tells me where Gary goes to yoga. I get there, no Gary."

"Oh fuck me," Vivian says, touching my thigh.

"I go down to Fatburger, place an order like it's my last meal, and there's Gary Oldman stuffing his face with a chili cheeseburger. I throw his ass in my car, race to LAX, pay for his ticket, one way, first class, Virgin Air, on my American Express card, and I don't leave until his plane takes off," I say.

"You da man, Josh," she smiles.

"Wait. It gets better. I get Arty on the phone in Cannes, tell him this amazing story, out of breath, how I got Gary on the plane and Arty says to me, 'So who else called?' I don't know who else called. I didn't have time to check messages, so he fires me on the spot and says—"

"'Stress less.' I know this story," says Vivian. "You're supposed to tell it with Tommy Lee Jones."

"You're stepping on my lines, Viv."

"So, Josh, you live nearby?"

We drive up Bronson Avenue in her brown Oldsmobile with its trash-filled backseat and WHAT WOULD SCOOBY DOO? bumper sticker. A mile up, her cell phone starts ringing to the tune of Sweet Home Alabama. Vivian makes me answer it and the Southern belle on the line asks me if I'm about to fuck her roommate. I say it looks that way, and recognize the voice as Lester's assistant.

"Is that Jessica? I need to talk to that bitch. Gimme the phone."

I realize the two women are having a conversation in Latin. Vivian cradles the phone over her chest, says Jessica's coming over. At a stop sign, Vivian yanks the parking brake. We make out, total strangers hungrily devouring each other like released convicts ordering a bucket of Extra Crispy at a KFC.

Outside Jerry's house, I start to freak. What if they find some of my brother's secrets? What if they think they belong to me? I'm not Jerry. I'm not even the keeper of his memory. This is not my shirt.

"I'm not leaving until we've used every one," says Vivian, wasting no time getting me inside her after laying out lines of banana coke and throwing a handful of condoms on top of Jerry's bed.

"Wow, love the view," Jessica says when she finally arrives, redheaded, green eyes, the kind of earthy beauty you'd find in a Girls of Starbucks Playboy spread, surveying the canyon from the sofa. Wearing only a belly button piercing, Jessica selects a screenplay from Jerry's library of favorites with magic marker titles on their spines harvested on a ceiling shelf. Jessica kisses Vivian on the lips and I say Hey, what about me, so she walks over and plants her wet mouth on mine. I put on Pink Floyd, thinking Shine on You Crazy Diamond would be appreciated more than In the Air Tonight. The girls do lines while I open a bottle of South African Merlot. Vivian and Jessica pay me absolutely no mind whatsoever. They just take turns fucking, sucking, and reading scripts.

In the morning I wake up alone and find a pair of lipstick kisses on my bathroom mirror. I blew off my flight back to Palmetto Dunes, as if I could afford to stay here until the Aetna life insurance check runs out, as if my life is now on the left coast, as if I have any idea what to do with myself. Detective Dupin calls to say she was going to question one of the bouncers from the Mink Slide but he left the country the morning after my brother was murdered. I find that significant, but she dismisses it as coincidence, saying his visa had expired.

"A month ago Jerry's office was moved to a building owned by the agency where the lawyers and accountants worked," says Dupin.

"Asbestos removal, that's what Jerry told me."

"Surveillance cameras and security guards only covered the main building."

"Which is why his office is now a crime scene," I say.

"You wanted to move out here?" She pauses. "Why?"

"To learn how movies get made," I say.

"You and everybody I know," she says. "Before he was an agent, your brother was a writer. Did you read any of his screenplays?"

"What's that got to do with the case?"

"Maybe he went to the office to get something from his computer. Maybe he was writing on the job," she ruminates and adds, "I'm writing one myself."

"You and everybody I know. How's that going?"

"I've been stuck on page 46 forever. Act Two is like the Grand Canyon."

"What's it about, detective?"

"It's about me, tracking a killer through the classifieds," she says.

"How does she catch him?"

"She doesn't. I want it to be open-ended, like Jack the Ripper," she says.

"Or the Zodiac," I say.

"Or the guy who really killed Kennedy—"

"What if he was the same guy?"

"What same guy?"

"What if like, the killer is the same guy from 1963?"

"He's from the past?"

"No, he's from the future," I say.

"Holy shit, that's genius, he can time-travel," she says.

"The guy is from the future, he's—"

"A time-traveling serial killer," says Dupin. "I've got to write this down."

"For centuries, innocents have taken the fall for his crimes," I say.

"The guy wants to be famous," she says.

"No, he wants to be infamous!"

"You should be my guru," she says. "We have to get the script to Lester Barnes!"

From the 26th floor in the Century City post-modern law office of Jerry's executor, Brad Blumberg, I'm staring at the careening JUSTICE FOR JANITORS demonstration outside the tower. Cops are breaking up the protest after they torched an effigy. I watch one of the Hispanic picketers step on the burning dummy and catch fire. The other janitors start stomping on him to put out the flames—Not Good. I go back to reading an unflattering New Yorker article about Lester Barnes. Jerry also got written up, a flick of madfame's tongue. As an agent, Jerry put movies together with Lester's clients and Omniscience's Independent Film Division by supplying scripts to producers, getting his fellow talent agents "pregnant with the material," then he presented a package of client combinations that were "not only irresistible to financiers and movie distributors but connected widely with audiences as well." The article went on to describe how Lester Barnes went through assistants like boxer shorts. Seven days a week (no overtime) they answered his never-ending phones, parked his Jaguar convertible every morning in the Omniscience garage, filled out his monthly farce called expense reports, and thanklessly curbed his dogs on the lawn of his superfluous Brentwood estate while he spent weekends at Two Bunch Palms with Miss July.

I wait for Brad to finish a call about "approvals" in a director's deal. When the "deal points" are done, the two callers tell a filthy joke, and hang up. Blumberg apologizes, asks if I would like a Vanilla Ice Blended. I say sure, no whip. The order is placed and some intern is sent flying.

"You get basically everything," says Brad. "In the event of the death of Jerry Albert Makos, the following decisions have been made, blah blah blah, joint assets shall be dispersed, couple of cash gifts to his friends, blah blah code purple, you get the residence on Aspen Drive, including all its contents, blah blah scholarship award established at USC film school in Jerry's name, based on academic excellence and personal performance towards his or her peers."

"Last wishes?"

"Scatter his ashes. I have the number to the helicopter service we use all the time, full bar, it's awesome," says Brad.

"Mind if I read the fine print?"

Brad shrugs, forks over the will.

"This says Arthur Livingstone and Lester Barnes are to guide the fund projects. Who's Arthur Livingstone?"

"He's a crumb snatcher—"

"Lester Barnes is also the notary," I say.

Brad's bald assistant, goateed and wearing glasses, interrupts us, urgently mouthing to his boss that someone of obvious significance can't wait any longer. Jerry's lawyer stands, extends his left hand in farewell.

"I've got to hop on this call," he says. "The Devil himself, can you believe it?"

Of course I'm nervous as I pull up in the Audi and my door is opened by a valet at Lester's Emmy party. I can already hear the din of cocktail conversation from the manicured front lawn as I pass candles that mark a trail to the front door of this Spanish hacienda. Private security guards check my name to see if I'm on their clipboard, and tell me to go right in. Is that Tony Soprano? I brush up against Wesley Snipes, overhear him bagging his agent, and bemoaning the fate of his futuristic X-treme sports/cop show he was producing because it got "yanked before we could find its audience." I turn directly at the star, pleasantly offer my condolences, and suggest Lester do his next deal. Wesley says he just signed on the dotted line and bumps my fist. I say something stupid like "Keep it real, mang." Wesley drinks his beer, turns directly away as if to indicate he does not know me. Moving on to a massive tented area lit up like a movie premiere, I'm paying more attention to the sheer number of recognizable guests than the magnificence of Lester's estate. Everyone's drinking champagne so I down two flutes back to back and enjoy the buzz. I ask for a third so I can walk around the grounds with something in my hand and not look as idle and nervous as I feel. Beyond the tented backyard, I can make out a tennis court in the distance, and a swimming pool with a security guard patrolling that area. He looks at me in a rather menacing way, which I write it off as boredom/doing his job. Through the glass windows of the game room, I watch a couple in their 40s, maybe 50s, playing pool. Champagne's making me tired, all that sugar. Mandrin, rocks, that's what I order from the actor-writer-bartender as I belly the bar. I make small talk with a kid who looks like he's somebody's son only to find out he's been hired by "Sony Animation" to save this "CGI family film" by doing some "punch-up work" on the script. I learn he used to be a speechwriter for Gore.

I point out an Oscar winning actress, amazed at the proximity. Gore Kid shakes his head: "I can still see her giving Lester a rusty trombone—Oh shit, Mo Reilly's here." I don't know what the name means, but the Gore Kid opens his cell phone and calls somebody to get a message to "Christian." Gore Kid tells whoever it is to tell Christian that his "new ex-wife" is on the warpath, and hangs up, satisfied that he has just performed some kind of civic duty. I snag a martini off a tray; turns out to be gin. I hate gin, but drink it anyway, burning my stomach lining, medicating because I feel so out of place here, unable to speak anyone's language. Is that Vince Neil? I introduce myself to a circle of guests having a hushed discussion of "Poor Maureen," who apparently eloped with Christian, whom she initially recruited from Joel Silver's company to do "comedy development" before being swept up in a "hot" two year love affair. Everyone, even "Tim Allen," knew about the happy "fuckbirds," yet no one expected Christian to pop the question. Two weeks after they returned from eloping in Guatamala, where he surfed with Brian Grazer and Matt Lauer and she spent her days getting pampered in the hotel spa, Mo gets an angry phone call. It's Christian's assistant, this 22-year old who says Christian just dumped her after she'd been having sex on the couch with her boss every Friday afternoon for the past two years like a standing dinner. The plot sickens. When Mo Reilly burst into a staff meeting to humiliate Christian and announce their marriage is over,

Christian replied, "in front of Les Moonves, " Surprise! They weren't really married in Guatamala; the paperwork was bogus; the sea captain who married them was a local witch doctor.

Christian only wanted to get Mo off his back until "pilot season was over." Mo resigned the next day and suffered a mental collapse. Now she's "trying to get into features." Navigating the back of the tent area, I'm clawing lobster quesadillas, Ahi tuna drizzled with wasabi, and garlicky snails when a TV camera crew rushes towards me. Flash of light blinds my eyes. What's happening? A boom microphone hangs over my head. I'm tackled by the Bug hugging me in his all-black Regis outfit—

"Watch out Hollywood," he says, "the Other Son Also Rises."

Camera lights blaze up, crew members point their equipment at the Bug, smiling at guests who see him as a walking, talking, burning three car pileup on the freeway. Is that Suzanne Somers? The dry cleaner explains he is financing a video journal called "Hollyweirdo" about his adventures in the screen trade.

"Can you believe this director? He sees a movie poster in one of my stores and says he has a script for me. Fluff n' fold guy reads it, says it has little action, no tits, bunch of zombies standing around talking," says the Bug.

Disoriented by the camera light, I feel an incredible need to flee.

"Socrates wanted to shoot it on super-16. I told him if I wanted to shoot a movie on film, I'd hire a real director. Only thing I'd pay him to direct would be a film about me. He caved, of course, because he's a pathetic loser who'd shoot a snuff film of his own mother on DV if it meant he could say Action!"

"Cut. Time to change the tape," says Socrates, horsey

face, tall, looks like Slash with long curly black hair dangling under a "Hollyweirdo" baseball cap. The Bug introduces us—

"This is Jerry's brother."

"You work in the Industry?" asks Socrates.

"What Industry?"

Reverting to pitch mode, Socrates starts telling me about Dead and Alive, his "Reservoir Zombies" project he intends to "start casting" and "shoot a fake trailer" and turn into a full length feature.

"Wow, sounds like you got it all worked out," I say.

"It was your brother's idea. Jerry was going to put up the money, take a presentation credit, and try to sell it after he quit the agency."

"Quit the agency?"

I can taste puke in the back of my throat—Not Good.

"Josh, I want to introduce you to Benny Pantera, a movie producer, one of my biggest customers," says the Bug.

Benny Pantera comes over, wearing a ridiculous purple Puma leisure suit, starts pumping my hand. I recognize Benny's name as one of the executive producers from the posters in my brother's garage—

"You produced The Mighty Mite," I say.

A few yards away, Benny's fucky companion, the bartender from the Mink Slide, ignores him, chatting with Barbara Streisand and James Brolin on a couch.

"Who's your date, Benny?"

"She's a barnacle looking for a ship," he says, unleashing a mortifying dog-whistle. Benny's date cringes, excuses herself, and skulks back to Benny.

"Siobhan, this is Jerry's brother," says Benny.

"I just heard," she sniffs, pinches her nostrils. "Sorry."

"We've met," I say. "The other night at the Slide."

"Nobody bothered to tell me. I mean, nobody," she says, meaning Benny.

Tent above our heads flaps with a Santa Ana, about to collapse, kill us all.

"Josh, if you ever need help with your own projects, script notes, financing, whatever, give me a call. Jerry and I were working on a few things together before, you know, his assassination—"

On the word assassination I spew all over Socrates and his DV camera. Siobhan scampers away. The Bug tries to clean the vomit off the lens with a napkin before giving up in revulsion.

"People are gonna wanna forget Hoop Dreams!"

Outside the bathroom door in the pool room, someone's racking balls on the table. I chug the bottle of mouthwash like a forty, swish the minty blue alcohol in my mouth, spit into the sink, bracing the sting, appreciating the numbness that lingers inside the hollows of my cheeks. I check for any vomit on my clothes, unlock the door and discover a red-haired, green-eyed beauty chalking her pool stick, lit cig in her mouth—

"Did you just hurl?" asks Jessica.

"On DV, no less. Where's Lester?"

"No idea. I'm off-duty," she says.

"Lester's sure got a lot of important friends."

"There's no such thing as friends in L.A., only people who have something you need."

"You know what bugs the shit out of me about this business?"

Jessica exhales, ashes her Winston, what?

"They got this thing in Daily Variety called 'Hitched,' right? Says who just got married. I've noticed most of these announcements are about people in the entertainment business. So and so is a vice-president of physical production at MGM; bride is the assistant event coordinator for Merv Griffin Productions. Every now and then, someone marries someone outside of movies, music, or TV. They call this person non-pro," I say.

"Right, right, non-pro. I hate that," she says.

"So basically, if Mother Theresa got married, they would say—"

"Hello? She's dead," she says.

"But if she was alive, maybe not a nun, if she married so and so in charge of original programming for the Discovery Channel, they'd say bride's non-pro," I say.

"Give me your left hand."

Her hands envelop mine. I'm jolted by their warmth.

"What are you, psychic?"

"You're going to end up quite rich, and successful," she says.

"Like my brother?"

Jessica drops my hand.

"That can't be good," I say.

Ominous stillness fills the room instead of an answer.

"You know what Jerry loved about this business?"

Jessica pulls open my belt, going for it, and she rolls down my pants to my ankles, kissing my hairy knees, which tickles, and I try to concentrate.

"You knew Jerry?"

"I used to be his assistant," she says.

She's licking parts of me I didn't know I had. Then she reaches around to cup my ass, and pulls me deep beyond, and the back of my brain explodes with an entirely new sensation, one for the books. Jessica almost nicks me, an unexpected withdrawal of her warm mouth replaced by a blast of cold air from outside—

"Bramley, no!" says Jessica.

I look over and see the eyes of a security guard and some hipster in a suit, open blue shirt, bushy black eyebrows.

"How could you do this to Lester?" asks Bramley.

"I'm not Lester," I say, pulling up my pants.

I notice a tableau of peering faces witnessing this highly embarrassing scene outside the window of the billiard room. Is that Anne Heche ? The rubberneckers are A-list, the jaws of life belong to Jessica, and the wreck is me.

"The girl stays, sir. If you'll follow me," says the security guard.

I am brutally escorted off the grounds by rent-a-cops when I happen to make brief, scintillating eye contact with Lester Barnes standing in front of his swimming pool, smoking a cigar, having a moment in the dark distance. I realize I am truly alone in this world, no blood tying me to anyone anymore in this chilly city where it's always sunny outside. No good can come from this expulsion. With tonight's discovery of a conspiracy, I extend my stay like a steely tourist.

Before his life was savaged forever, Jerry and I were driving around looking for a parking space until we found one in a bank across from the Silent Movie Theatre on Fairfax. SYPHILIS-MAKE-A-WISH said the marquee above the theatre—

"I'm making out with her in the booth at Vida, first date, bill comes to like, 175 dollars. I decide to take it slow, get to know her better a little, why not? Third date we're in the Chrysler, I'm trying out this side of me that's all affectionate and sweet, saying these stupid things. I'm not looking at her like the usual furry hole. I'm getting emotionally invested, this funny weird vibe, but good. I start thinking in the car: I am going to marry this bartender chick," said Jerry.

"Strike one right there," I said.

"Then she tells me she was molested," he said.

"Which means she was raped," I said. "Who was it, her daddy?"

"Daddy was a deadbeat. It was the babysitter."

"Still a hole in one, though, right?"

"I don't even get to putt for birdie. I suggest going back to her place, and Siobhan says 'We can't, my mom just moved in, and she's stopped having her period!'"

Outside, a scruffy doorman with dark glasses spoke into his cell phone with an Irish lilt, recognized my brother, nodded curtly, and lifted up the velvet rope. Into the lobby, where b/w photos of Dietrich, Keaton, Chaplin, Douglas Fairbanks, Jr. and Mary Pickford hung on the spider-webbed walls. I received a goody bag with party favors: a studded black leather cock ring, flavored condoms, joy jelly, a petite vibrator, battery included, a CyberWhore.com DVD, and pink gumballs called Pussy Drops—

"You can't stay with me, bro, I need my space. How do you plan on making rent when you're out here?"

"I could be a tennis instructor, maybe bartend a little. What about reading?"

"Nobody fucks the reader," he said. "Faith Don't Leave."

"What about it?"

"We're in an elevator. You have two minutes, pitch me."

"OK, script opens with a boat sinking and a young woman named Faith walks into a San Diego psychiatric hospital where she tells her shrink she's going to kill herself on her 18th birthday. Doc has 24 hours to prevent the kid from killing herself and unravel the mystery. In the end, turns out Faith was involved in a boating accident on her birthday that killed her parents and fiancé. The doctor isn't real, there's no psychiatric hospital. The twist is the whole movie is what flashes through her mind before she forgives herself and joins them in death."

Big-titted waitress offered me a watermelon shot.

"What makes it great?"

"The script begins on page one. The story stayed a mile ahead of me. The ending left me breathless. And, it's about redemption."

"What's the tone?"

"Very Wizard of Oz," I remember saying to Jerry.

"That's exactly what the director said after I sent it to him."

"So when do I start at Omniscience?"

"Road to Hell, Josh. Road to Hell," he said.

"What do you mean?"

"One day you will look back on your decision to enter the movie business with nothing but sadness and regret."

"That's you talking, bro. I know what I want," I said.

"I'll make a few calls," he said, but I didn't believe him.

Inside the boxing gym on Vine and Santa Monica, a chill filters the air from the second story mini-mall's open windows. A boom box with a pile of CDs boots out a bass line of Latin Hip Hop. A filthy mirror runs alongside the entire wall. I go over to a tall, gaunt African wearing a dark green hooded sweatshirt: K.O. BOXING—IT TAKES BALLS TO RULE THE WORLD.

"You the pro, aintch you?" asks the African.

"They call me Josh," I say.

"I saw you at the memorial service," he says.

"You must be Terrondus," I say.

I ask how much to join. Terrondus says five bucks a day or fifty a month. My hands tense into fists. I need to start wrapping. I slap a five into the trainer's palm. I change into my brother's workout clothes, knuckles taped, body ready for punishment and release. Bearded Russians shadowbox, moving around in a circle, throwing punches—

"They arrested anybody yet?"

I shake my head.

"No justice, no peace," says the African.

"I think the detective on the case cares more about selling her script than catching the guy," I say.

"How do you know it was a dude?"

"What do you mean?"

"Life ain't nothing but bitches and money," he says.

Terrondus and I notice a toothpick-thin Chinese chick on the treadmill wearing a T-shirt that says GOT TITS?

"Leggo my egg roll, she's mine. C'mon, boy, let's hit the mitts."

I find a pair of blue 16 oz gloves and put the left on first. With my other hand taping the Velcro tight around my wrist, I read the warning label. I put the other glove on, pull the strap over my wrist with my teeth, throw a few punches, roll around my neck, and stalk Terrondus along the ropes. The African plants his feet, offers a red leather mitt and barks—

"Jab! Double Jab! One-Two! Double Jab, Upper Cut, Left Hook, Right Hand!"

Hundred and eighty seconds later, bell rings. I'm panti-ng, holding up my left glove, pointing to the warning label.

"What's ding death?"

"Get outta my face," says Terrondus, waving his mitt.

I make him examine the label and he doesn't know what ding death is, or how you get it. Terrondus shows the warning label to other fighters. I hear a shout of laughter.

"What's the fucking punchline?" I ask the fighters.

"I think the word is inclu-ding."

I look down to address the unexpected owner of the explanation, all five beautiful feet of her. Curly black hair, olive skin, midriff exposed under a T-shirt: IFITY-WYBMAB? She has a diabolical rack.

"Say that again?"

"There's a hyphen on your glove. Here, see?"

I have this unbelievable ache to kiss her. IFITY-WYBMAB holds up her left glove to show me the label:

"BOXING IS A HAZARDOUS SPORT. MANUFAC-TURER ACCEPTS NO RESPONSIBILITY FOR ANY INJURIES, INCLUDING DEATH, NECK INJURIES AND/OR PARALYSIS."

Later, I pull up in the Chrysler while IFITYWYBMAB

waits at a bus stop.

"So what does your shirt mean?"

"If I Tell You Will You Buy Me A Beer?"

"Hop in," I say.

To my surprise, Carmen Coronado makes like a bunny and joins me in the front seat. She opens a lunch box from some funky store in Echo Park, revealing her mom's empanadas. Vermont and Wilshire, I drop her off at a subway station, where we bump fists goodbye.

"Hey star!" says a girl in her 20's-maybe, waving me over at Hu's on National. She's sitting across from a severe-looking fifty year old woman in a dark suit. I have no idea who they are, but I'm curious so I make my way over to their table steaming with plates of pan-fried noodles.

"Aren't you Jerry's brother?" asks the 20-something, who has a fucked up left eye like Detective Columbo.

"They call me Josh," I say.

"That was some party at Lester's the other night."

I'm about to ask her how she knows—

"It was all over the trades," she says, moving her tongue up and down against the inside of her cheek, an obscene round of charades.

"I'm Serena Stern. This is my boss, Orly Gold, of GMG," she says.

Serena must be the daughter of the bastard son of a thousand maniacs . It's not just her weird eye that makes it hard not to stare. On the left side of her face, something worse than crow's feet, more like second-degree burns.

"Eating on Fox today. We just wrapped Sgt. Stranger. You read, right?"

"Top of my pile," I lie.

"Orly read the original at Swarthmore and always felt The Stranger was a cop movie waiting to happen. I said to Orly, 'Hey, I went to film school. I didn't have to take any of those classes.'"

Orly is staring at me like I'm the burn victim.

"Take a Polaroid, it'll last longer," I say to Orly.

"I almost feel like I'm looking at a ghost," she says.

"Why, because I almost look like Jerry?"

"I used to read scripts for him," she says.

Serena gasps.

"Don't take this the wrong way Orly," I say. "You don't exactly look like a reader."

"Well, back then, I certainly looked like someone going through a divorce, restraining order, kicked off the Sony lot, the whole bit. Jerry didn't ask me to do a test script, which I appreciated," she says.

"Is that right?"

"When Rothman greenlit my project, Jerry finally told me what I wanted to hear, something he said he always wanted to tell me."

"Which was?"

"'You're fired.'"

"You made Page Six, Josh. Now everyone knows who you are," says One Eye. "Party tonight at the Peninsula, you should come."

Orly places her business card in my hand.

"Josh, if you ever come across a really good script, something you think I should take a look at, give me a call."

"What makes you think I know anything, Orly?"

"DNA."

Serena's deluxe suite is teeming with so many pajama people, so obviously in the movie business, it feels like Jerry's world. I instantly want to belong. I'm collecting everybody's business cards as One Eye greets the acquaintance party like close family members: Ivan (works for Bruckheimer), Pepper (used to be Christina Ricci's personal assistant), Talley (manages that kid from the Tarzan N the Hood movie), and Ike (Korean-American, pledged CAA, currently works for Abrams and Associates).

"Abrams?" asks Serena. "What is that, a nanny agency?"

A subtitled German film with a red-haired woman named Lola jogging plays on a large TV screen accompanied by a Dylan-esque song from the hotel room's CD player. I'm enjoying the song's melody, when some girl holding a potato chip with garlic dip in front of her mouth points out the song by David Gray is called "Babylon." I thank her for noticing me.

"You're welcome Jerry," she says.

I don't bother to correct her. Potato Chip ambles her way to Serena's circle when some guy grabs her ass and squeezes really hard. Potato Chip's face scrunches up in pain, then she laughs, spewing dip & chip into her hand. She catches the regurgitated food and palms it back down her gullet. Serena says something to Potato Chip, who gasps loudly. Mortified and embarrassed, she is now making her way over to me—

"I'm so sorry. I just heard the news. I've been in Europe

for two years. Who did it, do they know?"

"Nobody knows anything."

"So what do you do all day?"

"I sit around and read scripts," I say.

Potato Chip doesn't introduce herself.

"You're a CE?"

"What's that?"

"You know the difference between a creative executive and a pound of bananas? A pound of bananas has a mind of its own," she says.

"I work out of my house in Beachwood," I say.

"Oh, you're a lit manager. No shame in that. Fish Called Wanda."

"I'm sorry?"

"Who directed it?"

"Who directed what?"

"A Fish Called Wanda," she says.

"You're not making any sense," I say.

"Charles Crichton. I'll pray for you."

Serena pulls me away, into a bedroom, onto the bed, where a group of bathrobed men and women are lounging around, taking bong hits, drinking beer, playing some sort of drinking/smoking game. The bedroom explodes with whoops and high-fives. I have no clue what just happened. The door to the bathroom is closed. Sound of toilet flushing. Laughter. Shrieking. Water in a bathtub sloshing, wetting the carpet by the door, a kind of fucking/fucking game.

"Heaven's Prisoners," says Ike, holding up an obscenely thick paperback Movie & Video Guide with a photo of Leonard Maltin on the cover.

"Phil Joanou," replies some girl in a pink sweatshirt.

"Destroy All Monsters!" shouts the Korean Torquemada, which is met with immediate protest, not because it's the title of a Godzilla movie, but because the film was released in 1968, way before the jumping-off point of 1980 established for the game. The room decides Korean Torquemada has to drink for his mistake and surrender the book. I learn you can call it "The Bible," or "Leonard Maltin," and nothing else, or you drink. The obese paperback gets thrown over Ike's shoulder, past outstretched arms and hits me in the chest. I catch Leonard Maltin, and look up at everybody in the room.

Ivan yells, "Throw out a movie at someone!"

I open Leonard Maltin at a random page, select a film from 1993, and lob it at Korean Torquemada.

"You. 20 Bucks."

"Keva Rosenfeld. Give me a hard one, dude," he says.

I open Leonard Maltin again. As soon as I see a movie with a year after 1980, I call out the title, expecting the name of a director.

"Amazon Women on the Moon," I say.

"Wait, wait, there were multiple directors on Amazon, you can't expect me to name all of them, duuude."

I am about to let Ike off the hook when some girl shouts out he has to name all of them or drink.

"I can do this: John Landis. Joe Dante. Peter Horton. Robert Weiss—"

Korean Torquemada falters, unable to name the last director. He hangs his head, beaten.

"Carl Gottlieb," I tell the room.

Everybody screams and watches the loser drink, exit in shame when the bathroom door opens, and two junior agents in soaked pajama pants and T-shirts with black letters spelling out Omniscience emerge with their freshly fucked concubine.

"What are you doing here?" asks Jessica.

"Playing Leonard Maltin," I say.

"I hate that stupid fucking book—"

Everyone screams and points at Jessica. Her hand shoots to her face, realizing she just called it a "book."

"You," I turn to Talley, "Paris Trout."

"Stephen Gyllenhaal, wait! You just gave me a cabler," says Talley.

Bible says the script by Pete Dexter debuted in the U.S. on cable. I not only have to drink, but now I'm facing my own inquisition. Talley doesn't want to hold Leonard Maltin, so he throws him to Jessica, who holds it up at me like a crucifix.

"Barton Fink," she says.

I should know this one, but for the life of me I can't recall the name of the director. I drink, knowing it means exile. I say goodbye to my executioner and add, in a whisper directly into her ear, "I'm not Jerry."

"That's for damn sure," says Jessica, closing her eyes.

Carmen Coronado lights up the smelly dark gym with her contagious smile when she asks me to spar with her. The bell dings, the round begins, and Carmen connects a right against my left temple. I see stars, flashes of white, close my eyes from the sting. I dance away from Carmen, galloping on the bouncy blue canvas, finding her in my vision between my fraying, taped headgear. Carmen's a mauler, shoves me against the ropes, tapping my kidneys. She's getting tired so I knock away her shoulder, step in, and smash her face. I immediately apologize.

"There's no sorry in boxing," she says, lunging at me with a right hook, which I block, and retaliate with a poorly-placed left. Ten second bell goes off. We come up to each other in the middle of the ring, throwing punches, swinging and ducking, connecting, shoving each other away until the round ends.

"I only fight women and children, keeps me sharp," I say.

"Esse, you need to work on more combinations. You've only got like, two moves. Get in shape, you gordo loco cavacho," she says.

Carmen wonders if I'm free tomorrow.

"Sure, let's hang out," I say.

In the Chrysler with the top down, Carmen Coronado tells me "chemo, not cancer," killed her mother. Then she tells me she doesn't have a car because it's at the police impound until she pays off her unpaid parking tickets. A boyfriend, Grover, is in prison for identity theft. After her uncle raped her, she left San Angelo, Texas on a one-way

Greyhound to San Diego, where she graduated from a Performing Arts school, moved to L.A., met Grover at a club that used to be called Spice but is now called something else.

Taking Beverly Glen, street lamps clocking above our heads, I hit Ventura and turn up Valley Vista Way when Carmen turns off her cell after discussing a fee with "Donald." I realize: I am driving around an actress.

"That your manager?"

"He's a pimp, not a manager. Turn here," she says.

"Where we going?"

"Audition in the Valley for some horror movie. It's 500 bucks for a topless, but there's a lot of dialogue which is good because I need the practice."

I wait in the Chrysler as Carmen heads for the audition at a warehouse off Tujunga Boulevard. I reach behind my seat to grab the script by Socrates Wolinsky about a gang of criminals who decide to go for "one last score" by robbing a monastery where the abbots have taken a vow of silence. The heist goes horribly awry, unleashing a virus that turns the monks into flesh-eating zombies. When Socrates called to ask me if I knew anyone who wanted to put up the money for the promo reel, I said I would write the check for the same deal he offered Jerry. Carmen exits the audition, climbs into the Chrysler, notices the script.

"What's that? Don't tell me you're in the business," she says.

"I read the trades," I say.

"You a writer or something?"

"Friend of mine's directing a short, says it's a fake trailer," I say.

"Can I read that script with you?"

"You can have it. I'll get another copy from the director," I say.

"No, I mean, read with me? You know, act it out in the car," she says, shimmying her shoulders.

"Get in the back," I say.

Seated at a table in the opening scene of Dead and Alive are MONK, a "ruggedly handsome" ex-priest turned criminal, sidekick LARRY ("think Tom Arnold"), and sexy femme fatale SKYLA, who translates for a mysterious Israeli Ecstasy dealer named GOVINDA who doesn't speak English—

LARRY whistles appreciatively at a b/w photo of hidden riches: "Goddamn, Monk. I ain't seen this much gold since we hit that crematorium in Whittier."

MONK, uncomfortable, flinches at the memory: "That's why we're doing this Larry, so we don't ever have to do that again."

GOVINDA mutters something.

SKYLA clarifies: "He says what you did is wrong. For someone who was once a man of God you should have more respect for the dead."

"Tell him, for a dead man he should have more respect for God."

Carmen looks at the script as if it were gold—

"What was your name again?"

"'He said what you did was wrong. For someone who was once a man of God, you should have more respect for the dead.'"

"'Tell him, for a dead man, he should have more respect for God.'"

We're parked in a mini-mall on Vineland before we head into the audition. Socrates and the casting director he's using are inside a rented casting space in a theatre next to a medical equipment store ("We Sell Blood-Cleaning Equipment"). In the Chrysler, Carmen's cell phone rings. She looks at the caller ID, sighs, and turns off her phone.

"Something wrong?"

"Grover's back. I kicked him out last night," she says.

"That was quick. How's he taking it?"

"Not Good—I think he's following me."

"Doesn't he know anybody else?"

"He's staying on people's couches, hooking up, but that's not gonna last forever. I thought he was going to rape me last weekend after he started this big seduction thing. I told Grover, don't even think about it—"

"Can I make a suggestion?"

"Go ahead, guru," she says.

I offer her a piece of paper with a name and #.

"What's this?"

"The name of Grover's parole officer. Dupin got it for me," I say.

"You think I should call?"

"I think Grover should know you have his parole officer's number. You mention the attempted rape, he's violated his parole," I say.

"You've given this some thought, haven't you Josh?"

"C'mon, let's go inside before the vampires see us."

Inside we find a card table with a clipboard and stapled script pages with magic markered scene numbers: #1 #3 #4. High-lighted at the top of every scene is a name: LARRY. MONK. SKYLA. Five women wait to be called, all dark olive skinned Mediterranean-types, holding up "Skyla" pages, memorizing their lines. Carmen goes to put on her makeup in the bathroom as I walk through a curtain and climb a short flight of stairs. There, behind a rectangular card table, eating falafel from Kosher Grill is Socrates, along with his casting director.

"Josh, this is my casting director Mandy," says Socrates. "Mandy, Josh is the lead investor."

"I'm the only investor, Socrates," I say.

"You're Jerry's brother. Did they catch the fucker yet?"

"Not yet," I say.

"Okay, who's next?" asks Socrates.

"Still waiting for your 4:00. She hasn't called to say she's late," she says.

"Throw her on the no-show pile," decides Socrates.

"Kelly's waiting down there. Let me go get her."

I feel out of place, like an intruder.

"I should get out of your way—"

"I need you to operate the camera. I really want your two cents on this. We're one Skyla away," he says.

The casting director re-appears, parting a brown tapestry with some Indian elephant ceremony design to reveal the next auditioning actress.

"Kelly, this is Socrates Wolinsky, the writer-director," Mandy says.

"Thanks for coming down. Kelly, this is Josh, he's

going to work the camera for us today," says Socrates.

"Before we begin, do you have any questions, Kelly?"

"Yeah, like, why am I with this guy Monk? It seems like this really dangerous thing to do, robbing a monastery?"

"Good question. See, to you, Monk is like your dad. You want his approval, yet you constantly think deep down he doesn't respect you. You hate him the way you hate your father, and you're doing this because ultimately, you want him to love you."

"Got it."

"Okay. Say your name and the role you're reading for. Camera ready?"

"Rolling," I say.

"Kelly Fortune. I'm reading for the part of Skyla," she says.

"Skyla, you're gonna read with me. Mandy's Larry," says Socrates.

"Wait. Can I stand?"

"Whatever makes you more comfortable," says Socrates. "Action!"

She sucks. So does the next girl. Flat and memorized. They are reading the words, not speaking them. Socrates introduces me as "the foreign sales guy." When they hear this, the actresses perk up like size queens. Next girl overacts badly, bombs her audition.

"Alright, throw her away," says the director. "Anybody else down there?"

"I don't think so. Let me go look," says Mandy.

A few seconds later, Mandy pushes through the elephant curtain with a big smile across her face like she'd just found a quarter in front of an expired parking meter. In walks Carmen Coronado, wearing a white T-shirt tied up in the front, silver crucifix necklace between her cleavage. Smoky eyes. Very light pink lip gloss. Torn jean shorts that barely cover her butt. Long lean legs. Sexy, simple rope heel shoes. Carmen acts as if we don't know each other. Socrates asks Carmen if she has any questions about her character.

"Yeah, is she a very religious person?"

"Not really. Why?"

"Maybe I'm reading into this, but I get the way she feels about Monk being an ex-priest. How she hates the Church, or maybe she just hates her Dad and Monk is this father figure. I think she doesn't know how she really feels about him so maybe this heist is how she's gonna find out."

Carmen puts away her pages and turns to the camera like she's done this a million times.

"Carmen Coronado. I'm reading for the part of Skyla."

I push a button. "Record" appears in my viewfinder.

"You know what fucks like a tiger and winks?"

In my viewfinder, Carmen winks.

"Action!"

After the grueling weekend shoot of Dead and Alive, I'm grateful to be with Carmen and Socrates at Sushi Nozawa on Ventura Boulevard. The star and director had really bonded on the set, although Carmen seems quiet tonight. As we wait for three spaces to open up at the sushi bar, Socrates can't stop talking about this horror film he's been hired to edit by some investor in Florida to try and make the deadline for the Sundance Film Festival—

"I'm cutting some crazy shit. These kids, the directors, nobody ever found them. Just footage this guy says was stolen from the evidence room at the police station. I'm supposed to cut all the hours and make sense of it. Parts of it are really fake; but if I get scared, I keep it," he says.

"Hours of what?"

"The Gainesville Evidence. Bunch of film school rejects at the University of Florida taped a hazing for a class project. Four pledges and two little sisters were ordered to spend the night in a condemned sorority house, eleven years after a mass murder, and given hand-held DV cameras."

"Little sister?" asks Carmen.

"Some eighteen year old DG pledge still clucking a retainer like she never left the tenth grade," says Socrates.

"And of course, it's haunted," I say.

"They can't leave the house all night, they're locked in. They're not allowed to go to sleep, if they get caught on camera taking a nap, they can't pledge until the fall. This guy who hired me thinks what's on the tapes is real."

I'm hot in the face. This sounds good. I know it's good,

and I'm trying to be popsicle cool. We are shown to the sushi bar. Signs behind Chef Nozawa say "Don't Even Think of Ordering a Spicy Tuna Roll," and "We Reserve the Right to Refuse Service to Anyone." Socrates reminds me not to directly address the sushi chef; I am expected to nod my head and express gratitude for the privilege of being admitted into Tunaworld.

"Socrates, I'm afraid to order hot tea," I say.

"Don't ask Nozawa," whispers Socrates, "for anything."

"Are we in Pyongyang or the Valley?"

I've never eaten sushi where my rice is served warm. I don't know what I'm eating but everything melts in my mouth. The line of people waiting for a table or a shot at the sushi bar runs outside the entrance door and spills into the parking lot. A single opens up at the bar. Charlize Theron, wearing a grey sweatshirt, nerdy glasses, sets down her Evian water bottle right on the sushi bar. Nozawa grunts six words to the fat woman who must be his oldest daughter. The hot towel is taken out of her hands before she can unfold it—

"Excuse me! I wasn't finished with that," says the Oscar-winner.

The Unagi Emperor calls his wife out of the kitchen, a scowling marine of a woman, and orders her to expel the transgressor. Everything is delivered in a short, grunting foreign language, playing out like a Japanese soap. Scowling Wife gently pulls the back of Charlize Theron's chair, indicating she must vacate the establishment.

"You've got to be kidding. I just sat down," she says.

Scowling Wife makes sweeping gesture that speaks: Please leave, before my husband Nozawa orders my head cut off with a sword after punch-out. Nozawa orders Charlize Theron to take her water bottle and leave.

Everyone stops eating, too afraid to take a bite.

Charlize Theron looks around the room full of collaborators, scrunched together at the tables and sushi bar: no one will come to her defense tonight.

"Hey everyone! He's making me leave!"

Eyes hug the floor, drop down to plates of sushi, anything but witness this absurd banishment. I'm about to comment when Socrates squeezes my leg so hard, I yelp. In the silence, Carmen, along with everyone else, shrivels up, shoulders hunched, protects their hills of pinkish ginger. I take another bite of my yellowtail, popping it into my mouth, licking warm rice off the back of my thumb as my brain explodes with sensation. I no longer care about the injustice of Charlize Theron's banishment. I only want Nozawa to serve me another exquisite piece of anything he decides to give me. Charlize Theron storms out, fighting tears—

"Fuck! I'm going to miss this place."

Socrates invited us to watch the new opening he's cut for The Gainesville Evidence, but I suggested a drink at the Mink Slide. Socrates didn't want to go, and Carmen jumped at the chance to view Gainesville, so now I'm going to the club by myself. Carmen walks out of Nozawa looking absolutely beautiful, eyes bright, contagious smile, curly locks of hair spilling over her shoulders. After hugs and high-fives with my people, the closest I have out here to calling friends, driving away I can't help but feel jealous watching Socrates escort Carmen to his Miata. I hit the steering wheel in anger. Heading south, I get off the 101 at Alameda. I turn right on Sunset until I hear the din of the Mink Slide from my driver's seat with the window down, driving past a bald bouncer holding a clipboard when I spot Siobhan leaving the club. I pull a U-y and follow the bartender being escorted to her car by another doorman wearing a vintage L.A. Gretsky jersey. I wonder where Siobhan lives. Let's see where she goes in her white Honda Civic.

I lose sight of Siobhan two times, as she navigates her coche east on Sunset which morphs into Cesar Chavez Boulevard, left on Broadway to catch the 110 North. Three cars behind and a lane over, I'm amazed at how well I'm doing. We go through the Pasadena Freeway tunnel and she cuts across a lane at the last minute to the 5. Horns blare. I keep the White Civic in my sights. Vrooming towards Glendale, she and I hit the 134 East together. I'm too close so I slow down, hide behind a couple cars. I turn the radio off so I can concentrate. Getting off at Avenue 64, I trail the Civic and watch her turn right at Doremus, taking Fortune Way into the hills of Glendale. Up we go, there's light traffic, which helps me, as Siobhan hasn't tried to shake me off her scent yet.

On Rutland Ave, I can see city lights distantly in my rear-view mirror. I sense she's going to a party with all the parked cars on the street, front wheels turned away from the curb. I can hear something like jungle drumbeats in the distance. Left on Larker, up Hillside Terrace, right on Kenworthy to Poppy Peak. Siobhan drives up to a white gate, rolls down her window to identify herself to a jar-head bouncer standing outside a Plantation-style house with huge marble columns and a chandelier above the front doors. Bouncer lets her park inside, speaking into a walkie-talkie to open the gates. I reverse down the street to look for a space. I'm so impatient I squeeze right up behind a Pathfinder and I know the parked ass of my Audi is blocking somebody's driveway but who's going to tow my car in the middle of the night? The gates are open as I walk up to the Plantation. I nod my head, walk right past the humongous black bouncer in his COUNTY MORGUE T-shirt.

"How you doin' tonite?"

His large hand grabs me by the neck.

"Man, that shit's so unnecessary. Siobhan here yet?"

"Password?"

I try to breathe, find the anger rising. I want to kill this man.

"I need a password," he says.

"Gianni Roastbeef," I say.

Morgue Guy releases my throat.

"A'ight, little man, go on in, enjoy yourself."

Heat lamps everywhere. The swimming pool is boiling with twenty or more naked women with plastic cups in their hands, making out with each other. There's a basketball court where an intense shirts n' skins game is happening in front of stands filled with spectators. Some of the players look like maybe they play for the Clippers.

They are filming inside the house. I can't get past the VIP rope to catch a sneak of whatever it is the lights and cameras are there for tonight. Away from the house, designed to distract and amuse the crowd, a high-on-ecstasy, friendly pair of funbags bounces naked on a trampoline. Someone hands me a joint, which I make a perfect pass with my fingertips to some guy dancing with a cornrowed albino chick when Siobhan walks right past me, makeup smeared, sweaty cheekbones. I keep dancing with myself, towards the backyard where I follow the bartender from the Mink Slide moving behind the basketball court to pace alone in a dark corner of the manor's railing, hundreds of feet above the canyon—

"Hey star," I say.

Siobhan snuffs, wipes her sleeve, coughs.

"How'd you get in? We're filming," she says.

"I heard something about you and a doorman," I say.

"Talk to Liam," she says. "Liam Everett."

A roar goes up after two points scored at the basketball court, coupled with DMX's "No Sunshine" over the loudspeakers.

"I heard Liam left the country," I say.

"Liam didn't do it."

"I'm supposed to just take your word for it?"

"Aw shit—Benny's calling me. I got to get back on set."

"I thought you said goodbye in your farewell interactive DVD."

Hair flitting across her face, Siobhan turns on her bare heel.

"Yeah well, rent's due and the check is in my mouth."

I wake up in the middle of the night, dehydrated, dying, throw the sheets off my naked body and head for the kitchen, drink from the faucet, gargle, and then spit into the dirty dish pile. I turn on a lamp next to an African statue, really just an elongated face that's cracked on the side, and there's a script on the coffee table. I make myself a triple Mandrin with the hopes that I'll black out on the couch and get back to sleep. I start on the first page of the Infamous script Dupin left for me. After the first sentence, I forget all about Liam Everett. By page 10, I have to put the script down because it's so tight, engaging, and quick. Her middle is a ride of car chases, carnality, serial killings, and time travel shoot-outs between a futuristic madman, a detective who reads like Dupin herself on the page, and her partner, a skip tracer from the future that delivers on our ecstatic story kibbutz. I put the script down and realize I'm near the end and I haven't stopped, not even to look at the page numbers. Dupin wrote the scary future stuff like she was from there. The moment feels holy, like I'm experiencing some greater design at work. Please don't drop the ball is my next thought as I return to the script's last 20 pages. And then she slays me by making the ending ambiguous and you don't know who went to the future happily ever after, but you hope it was the good guys, and you won't let yourself admit that maybe, somehow, the time-traveler had won. I can't believe how blessed I feel. This one will definitely sell. I wish Jerry was alive. He would know what to do next.

Inside a bungalow at Crossroads of the World, Socrates

types in some commands, the disturbing opening credits of a promo reel of Dead and Alive strobes across our faces. Over black, I hear screaming, then gunfire. We are running, hand held, in downtown L.A. Shot of Carmen as "Skyla," raising her pistol and firing at something off-screen. Then it cuts to a startling pop-up zombie closeup, whose shotgunned head splatters gore—

"What's going on with Gainesville?"

"Got into Sundance, bro, midnight screening."

"Congratulations, Socrates! I mean, holy fuck!"

"If we go," he says.

"What do you mean, if? You're going. I'm fucking driving you to the festival if I have to," I say.

"I'm ready to go, but this idiot from Florida, he's out of money. I haven't gotten paid. I'm thinking about maybe holding the masters hostage until I find nine people to borrow ten grand each and buy the film," he says.

On screen, a digital clapper snaps, numbers freeze, gets pulled away, revealing an ice rink where "Skyla" and "Monk" skate into each other's arms. Carmen "slips," Monk catches her in an embrace, and their heads come together in a soulful kiss. Hand-held camera, on the ice, skates right up to them at mid-rink. On screen, the lovers' kiss continues endlessly before I hear myself scream: "Cut! Cut, Goddamn it cut!" Camera whirls around to find me on the set, having blown my cool.

"Put me down for ten," I say.

"Josh, you haven't even seen it."

"Maybe I can bring an investor who'll write a check for the whole thing."

"I'm telling you, Josh. No bullshit. Gainesville is gonna make Siobhan's footjob gangbangs look like Aladdin."

I'm playing Canadian doubles on a grass court, crushing Lester Barnes and his doubles partner, some marketing executive from MGM, who doesn't seem to object to Lester chasing drop shots, hitting baseline winners while screaming on the phone—

"Sell the fucker. What do I mean? I mean 'sell it!' I can't carry you anymore. This has got to stop. I gave you Liza, didn't I? Don't ever call me again for assistance. You're too fucking old to be living out of a car. Don't tell me to lower my voice of course we're on a secure line! Quit being so fucking paranoid! No, I will not come down to the men's shelter. Why? Because that's skid row, man! Find an alley. Don't go in there Arthur! Why? That's where bums get raped, dumped into the toilet hole. I know because I saw a news segment by that reporter I fucked at the Cheer Fever premiere—Hello? Arthur?"

MGM excuses himself to take a leak. Lester resumes the conversation he and I were having at the net—

"Josh, I can't get it up with people I care about."

"They got intimacy clinics for that."

"If I wanted intimacy, I'll visit my mother. Let me tell you something, Josh. I won't mention his name, but Arthur Livingstone is a disgrace to agenting. A disgrace. He has lost everything. Lives out of his Porsche, which he refuses to sell and get an apartment because he feels the need to keep up appearances. What does that tell you? What meaning can you derive?"

I shrug, inhaling this guy's carbon.

"As an agent, Arthur never learned to be a human being.

He made the mistake of confusing his career for a life. Don't ever make that mistake."

"I won't."

"Perception is everything in this business. You can be Oz the Great and Terrible, but never let the nitwits see you for the hideous dwarf you really are," he says.

"Hey Lester, I read a script called Infamous I want to produce."

MGM returns to the grass court with a six-pack of Milwaukee's Best—

"Did you guys ever see Siobhan in that disgusting bukkake she did?"

"Josh, could you live with MGM buying this script for a hundred grand? Another hundred and fifty for the writer if it gets made, half that for shared credit," offers Lester.

"But you haven't even read the script," I say.

"Lester, you want in on this?" asks MGM.

"What do you say, Josh? You're bringing me your project."

"I don't know, Lester. Do you want in?"

"Make sure Josh here gets an Associate Producer credit, his own card, front of the film, all paid ads, twenty five thousand dollar development fee up front now."

"Mighty generous of you, Lester," says MGM.

"Alrighty then," says Lester. "We'll get Blumberg to crayon the deal."

MGM: "Perfect."

Lester: "Whose serve?"

They get up to play tennis as if I'd said "Yes."

"Wait! Brad's my lawyer, he can't represent everyone in this deal," I say.

"Twenty-five thousand for a handoff isn't enough, Josh?" asks MGM.

"I'm not signing anything until Lester reads the script."

"Josh, I don't like to leave a big bag of money on the table," says Lester.

"What bag of money? What table?"

"Tell you what, Josh, Monday morning call my office and we'll send a messenger to pick up the script," says Lester.

"You'll read it Lester? Don't give it to your assistant."

"I'll read it on the treadmill."

Panochitas Gorditas #22 plays in the background while I slip into costume before my date for the evening arrives. Going through my brother's mail I found a sinister invitation to a Halloween party: a black postcard with silver ink, addressed to Mr. Makos, and a number to call for directions. I'm wearing Jerry's silk boxers and black Armani T-shirt. I open a protective suit bag and withdraw Jerry's banana yellow suit. Inside Serena Stern's silver SUV, she's wearing the dumbest costume: bloody bandage over her left ear, palette and brush, with a paint-flecked jumpsuit.

"Who are you supposed to be?"

"Somebody almost famous," I say.

"You look like a typical Hollywood asshole," she says.

"Really? Typical. Even with this?"

I reach into my jacket pocket and withdraw a Tiffany silver card case. I slide out one of my brother's Omniscience business cards to Serena, who doesn't get the joke. As we circle the party on Fountain, Serena can't believe there's no valet parking, which she says is a sign that no one important will be there. We find a space near Santa Monica and Sycamore, park and walk warily north with Serena complaining every step of the way. The more she opens her mouth the more I want to get the hell away from her. All she does is talk shop. I regret using my invite on Serena by the time we get to the house on Fountain and face the USC linebacker with helmet and clipboard behind the velvet rope. I say my name is Jerry Makos. Serena ditches me before I can eject her. Ivan from

Bruckheimer remembers me from the Peninsula and asks if I have anything I think he should read.

"Hey Jerry, thought you were dead," asks a stranger dressed as Gandalf.

"Stop reading the trades," I fire back.

The exterior of the house itself is the height of ramshackle chic: dirty, wooden, a long porch, surrounded by shrubbery and tall trees, very Hansel and Gretel. Band outside, thrashing grunge, singer sounds kind of like Blind Melon. Glow in the dark bracelets and necklaces adorn most of the women. I push past unfamiliar loungers, a pungent mist of grin hangs over us like a college campus cloud. I order a Stoli Vanilla cran, exit the outdoor bar with a precious plastic Dixie cup. Costumed freaks come up to me like I'm a celebrity, react to having Jerry back in their lives, quick to give me their business cards. I wave hello at the leering Gore Kid, done up as Johnny Depp channeling Ed Wood. Across the human traffic, there's Mo Reilly behind the band's stack of speakers, being felt up by someone, I can't see who just yet, because this Belushi guy wearing a sweatshirt ("College") acts like he knows me and starts pitching me this lame idea that's "Angel Heart with a clone." Mo Reilly is kissing a woman, dressed as Private Benjamin. I start to get aroused watching them until Serena Stern slips her arm under mine and decides to take me for a moonlight stroll. I feel myself go soft. Serena announces Ivan just told her about the spec I'm going out with and she wants me to "slip it to her." Ridiculous exchange of cheap repartee/scamming ensues. I look directly into Serena's fucked up eye.

"That's all we ever talk about. No one talks about anything else," I say.

"We don't have to talk at all—"

"I mean, it could be plumbing. 'Nice plumbing.'

'You're a plumber? I'm a plumber!' 'I saw the best pipes last night at the Grove.'"

"Whatever, Josh. How is this script I hear everybody's tracking?"

"What script?"

"How'd you like to spend a minute in me?"

Serena's ass fills up the sink, screaming she's getting wet by the faucet that's running accidentally because of her elbow, people outside pounding on the bathroom door. Flash and I'm fucking Serena on the set from one of Jerry's CyberWhore.com DVDs, her head hanging over the diving board, hair floating in the water.

"How's my minute?" I ask, pumping into her, "How's my minute?"

"Almost up. I'll tell you when," she says.

Flash and Serena's now a zombie from Dead and Alive, so I switch-fantasize to Carmen, imagining her legs draped over my wrists, holding them up during my precious minute—

"Rampart Police! Open this door! Right now! LAPD!"

Serena pushes me away. Still wearing the condom, I yank up my pants, steady my feet. Outside the door, people are running and screaming. The band stops playing. We stand there, cold, wet, nothing to say to each other. Over the sound of water running in the sink we hear someone shout—

"Nice costumes you assholes!"

Outside our door, the party explodes with laughter. Serena's eyes widen, realizes the bust was only a prank.

"You've got your brother down," she says. "You fuck just like him, all over the place."

I look away. When I turn back to the doorway, my frame is missing a person. I step into the hallway and come face to face with a raised 9mm pistol and an instantly recognizable Actor wearing an LAPD costume—

"Who are you supposed to be, some kind of slick Hollywood Asshole?"

"Hey, I know you," I say.

"You do? From where?"

"We got drunk together once at—"

"Whoa, I don't like the sound of where this is going."

"Martini Shot! Martini Shot!" I say.

"Shh! Shh. Not so loud, easy there, little buddy."

I mention I heard his show won best drama series. Actor from the Mink Slide says he's on a completely different TV show, and somberly adds he recently "lost" his manager. I feel for the guy, thinking somebody died, when Actor explains his advisor is missing, lost on a safari with Katzenberg, probably eaten.

"No more Lion King jokes. I heard you got an Emmy at Lester's party."

"It was definitely a performance," I say.

"You're a funny guy, what do you do again?"

"I'm a plumber."

"Right on. So you remember that one-act I told you?"

I proceed to recount the entire play to Actor, whose face sprouts amazement as I pretty much recite, verbatim, his dream project.

"You're incredible. Do you have a card?"

I give him one of Jerry's business cards.

"Send me your play. I'll read it on the treadmill."

"You can be my manager! You've got to help me find out who I have to fuck to get off that TV show! Maybe if I have the courage to dump my bitch girlfriend and quit drinking, Hell, I might even one day write the feature and you'd get to guru the whole thing. Excuse me, I've got to find my partner, Rafael Perez."

Backyard: someone has built a huge bonfire that shoots

flames straight up into the sky. People tripping on Ecstasy dance around a poetry slam given by a curly-haired guy wearing a Melrose Larry for President T-shirt and coke-bottle glasses—

"This is where 40 degrees is considered freezing!" says Melrose Larry.

The party is still going off, but the vibe has thickened, turned dark and sour, black smoke churning from the fire, costumed guests and clowns coughing, puking, pissing by the sides of the house.

"This is where we spend more time in our cars than we do in our homes!"

Swirling blue/red police lights fill up the backyard. People head for the exits, worried for their careers. Back fence gate is thrown open by a guy dressed as Freddy Krueger, who gestures to a bunch of costumed Charlie's Angels to flee with a flick of his finger-knives.

"This is the city where lots of untalented people get somewhere! This is the city where lots of talented people get absolutely nowhere!" says Melrose Larry.

I look into the window of the house and see a uniformed police officer in the kitchen unhook his gun holster. In the next room, Actor from the Mink Slide decides to whip out his hand cannon. Police Officer reacts—

"This is the place where the cops are the criminals!"

Three gunshots hurt my ears. Actor crumples to the floor.

"This is the place where we have stars in our eyes and tears in our souls!"

Circle of Actor's friends are dappled with martyr's blood.

"And this is where I prefer to be!"

I ask Jessica if she thought my brother was a burn-out case as we enter the Hollywood Bowl carrying a basket of South African Merlot, sandwiches from Bay Cities (Jessica's idea), stoned wheat thins (desert island favorite for me), and a thing of Fontina cheese.

"I think a few cylinders were shot, definitely," she says.

Of course Lester's box is first class, rock star decadent. We take in the majesty of the florescent amphitheatre, complete with an impressive symphony orchestra.

"When you worked for Jerry, did you ever take a call from a guy named Liam Everett?"

"Name sounds familiar. Is that the director who brought the rabbi and the priest to the meeting at New Line after Ed Norton locked him out of the editing room?"

Jessica takes out a cigarette that's actually a one-hitter pipe. She fires it up as darkness falls and our only light is the stars. I try to read the program on my lap, but I can only make out the words "Impresario" and "Clarinet." I figure I'm in for a long night, so I suck hard on the pipe, cough myself purple, and hand the THC-delivery device back to its owner, who starts clapping wildly.

"Lester's lying low," I say.

"Peter Bart mentioned his trip to Mumbai with Swami Bhagavita."

"Is that good?"

"If you're a member of the Academy, I guess," she says.

An elderly white haired man resembling Brother Theodore enters stage left to applause. He milks it like tonight is his last night on Earth. The clarinet player walks on stage to a staggering detonation of clapping, even more raucous than the first display. Clarinet whips out a silk handkerchief, stuffs it into the mouthpiece, pulls a piece of string from the other end, and threads the entire hankie through the instrument.

"That's for the spit," Jessica informs me.

The audience erupts again as two fat sopranos walk on stage decked out in plunging necklines and blinding jewelry. The orcas are joined onstage by a rail thin tenor and a midget-sized baritone. The one-act opera seems to be about a producer struggling with rival sopranos who audition for the leading role. Shenanigans ensue. The maestro tries to calm down the bitches in an absurd, over-the-top trio. Finally it is the words of the cheerful, blissed-out final quartet that really gets to me. The divas agree not to have the other one killed by their foot soldiers. The impresario agrees to produce an opera with two leads for harmony's sake. Baritone is thrilled, but demands everything in writing. At the finale, everyone's onstage, belting out lines how "every artist strives for glory and applause" and "bows to fame," but every artist should "learn" that fame is something one must "earn" and be "worthy of acclaim." That's the "name of the game."

"They promoted five agents last week at Omniscience," she says.

"Anybody we know?"

"Vivian went straight to the CFO's office and threatened to sue for sexual harassment courtesy of Lester Barnes if they didn't promote her with the other trainees."

"Did they?"

"Bastards sent her back to the mailroom. Then they put her in Dispatch, running errands and messengering scripts in a jalopy with no air-conditioning."

I raise my middle finger. "Complaint department is one

flight up."

"My God, you don't give a fuck about anything!"

"Shut up, I do too."

"Like what? Come on, what do you care about?"

"Why are you busting my chops over this?"

"Because it's all about passion, Josh, this business is about passion, don't you get it? I'm trying to figure out if you have one passionate stem cell in your brain. Just what exactly are you about? Do you matter! Are you someone's reason to live?"

I show Jessica what I am capable of in the moment. I hold her face with my hands and kiss her cold, cracked lips with whatever emotion I have left to give. I break the kiss, pull back, snail-like, and crack open my eyes.

"I see," she mutters, dead.

I kiss her again. This time, she responds, and I'm not exactly sure why.

"Goddamn, I love your view."

"I'm ready to put the house on the market. Lester gave me the name of his crazy real estate lady—"

Jessica disappears into the kitchen.

"Got anything else besides quarts of Mandrin, Josh?"

"You guys drank all my wine last time."

"Who?"

"You and Viv. Come back here, why am I shouting in my own house?"

"Get off the couch and make me a vodka something."

In the kitchen, I remove the milky white gallon of Mandrin from the freezer, expelling whispers of frost from a hellish ice wasteland; take out two Tiffany glass tumblers, shove them full of crushed, lime-flavored nuts of ice from the bag; wash a large steel martini shaker, squeeze lime juice, pour the Mandrin, cranberry and mango juice, and proceed to dole out two frothy, dark magenta-filled Lava Lamps.

"To Jerry," offers Jessica, "you bastard."

"Why bastard?"

"Because he could be. Most of the time, and not just to me."

We clink, splashing vodka over our hands and wrists. We both switch glasses over to the other hand and greedily lick ourselves clean of drink.

"Was my brother evil like Lester Barnes?"

"Calling Lester Barnes evil is giving that pig way too much credit."

I point to a framed poster with a woman on all fours,

wearing fishnet stockings, offering her ass to the world, under kidnap block letters: "MAKE FRIENDS THE HOLLYWOOD WAY—FUCK 'EM!"

"Omniscience made Jerry take down that poster because they said it created a 'hostile' work environment."

"Man, you'd think the agents would dig it," I say.

"When you live in Hollywood, you fuck first, get it out of the way, then you're friends," she says.

"So was Jerry a real bastard?"

"You don't want me to bad mouth your brother now, do you?"

"Go ahead, spill."

"He stole a writer's idea, gave it to a writing team client and they sold it to Universal for $800,000."

"Is that as horrible as it sounds?"

"It's pretty horrible," she says.

"I'd be fucking furious. You never got a phone call from the writer?"

"No threatening postcards, nothing."

"Sounds like you two got away with it."

"Jerry gave me five grand as a year-end bonus. He even wrote 'Blood $$$' on the envelope with the hundreds inside."

"What a guy. Did you ever think about telling this story to the police?"

"Never crossed my mind."

"Cross your mind? Jesus Christ, Jessica, did you even think? What were you looking for that night you and Vivian came over?"

"A good time."

"Scripts? All you did was scripts."

"That's not all we did."

"Lester sent you, didn't he?"

"I fucking John Williams'd the whole thing. Lester said he'd promote us if we brought him Jerry's novel, but we didn't find it. I never believed he was writing one," she says.

"Why not?"

"I thought it was bullshit, a rumor, something that fed the legend."

As soon as I wake up, I see three torn, ribbed Sheik wrappers next to the bed and realize we probably passed out. I walk out naked to find Jessica when I hear the sound of slapping skin and grunting. Reflected in the TV screen, Jessica's on the couch, topless, wrapped in a blanket, touching herself, eyes widening at an advertisement for CyberWhore.com showing a grass tennis court orgy where hundreds of men and women are fucking, eating potato chips, grilling hamburgers and hot dogs. Sensing my presence, Jessica waves me into her blanket nest, surprises me with a good morning kiss.

"Come back to bed, Jessica. Staff meeting."

"I like watching some of this stuff. I found the DVD in a goody bag," she says.

"I'm not familiar with her work."

On TV: a mascara-smeared Siobhan inside an adult bookstore, surrounded by so many naked men it's difficult to count. Jessica throws me the remote and goes to make coffee.

"Tell me if you see Lester," she says.

I'm back in the adult bookstore with the fellahs. I look for Lester, scanning all those red faces. On screen, I see Jerry for the first time in ages. He's in Siobhan's mouth.

I pull into the cavernous garage of Omniscience, past a guy standing outside with a cardboard sign: WILL SCREENWRITE FOR FOOD. A traffic jam of BMWs, Range Rovers, and Porsches down the ramp. WILL SCREENWRITE FOR FOOD seizes the opportunity to penetrate the garage and plead his case with agents when the detective on my brother's case calls my cell phone—

"Any word yet about anything?"

"Don't quit your day job," I say.

"Why do you say that?"

"I can't get anybody on the phone," I say.

Two dark suits appear at the bottom of the ramp. Another Omniscience security guard appears at the mouth of the garage. WILL SCREENWRITE FOR FOOD drops his cardboard signage, opts for a running slide across an agent's Merc, creasing the 450 SL hood. In my rear-view mirror, WILL SCREENWRITE FOR FOOD eludes his pursuers out of the garage, spastically crosses the street, and collides with a roach coach just before it announces its arrival to the assistants with a cheesy musical horn blast.

"Your brother had quite a matrix going on," says Dupin.

"The bouncer, the bartender, the assistants, Lester Barnes, Benny Pantera. Am I forgetting anyone? Are you sure everybody checks out?"

"People didn't want your brother dead, people wanted him around. How did Jerry feel about you moving out here? Was he supportive?"

"Very supportive, he paid for my rehab," I say.

A crowd forms around the yellow POLICE LINE DO NOT CROSS tape that borders the agency from WILL SCREENWRITE FOR FOOD, lying face down in the gutter. An agent crosses the street, eager to start dealing as soon as he gets in, and in full view of cops and paramedics, viciously flicks his lit cigarette at the corpse.

"So what's this I hear about you and Jerry having a knock-down drag-out fight outside the Silent Movie Theatre?"

"Who told you that, Siobhan?"

"I need you to be straight with me, Josh."

"No, you want me to confess. Confess to what, that we weren't close? That we didn't talk that often?"

"Was he worried about paying for another rehab? Did he have a problem with you moving out here?"

"Jerry told me to stay out of the Industry and go back to Palmetto Dunes."

"I heard you punched him," she says.

"He kept saying he was doing me a favor."

I enter the lobby and react to a truly hideous painting. Three female clowns man the reception desk surrounded by ostentatious flower arrangements and brownie baskets. One woman is all chest, no face; the other looks like a Demoiselle d'Avignon. I tell the Picasso I'm here to see Mr. Nikolovski. Harpy receptionist at Omniscience flashes her shark teeth, clacks her Guinness Book of World Records-freaky nails to get my attention and leads me to an office on the first floor. I swung this meeting with Nikolovski, whom I've never met, after I said it was personal, urgent, and about Jerry. I was told I could have five minutes.

Nikolovski's office theme is Hawaiian: LILO & STICH autographed poster, framed Hawaiian shirts, longboard in the corner. Nikolovski himself could use a tan.

"Sorry I wasn't at the service. I was being deposed by the Gang of McIntyre."

"Sounds scary."

"They call me the Agent of Death around here."

"I thought that was only around Christmas."

Nikolovski offers me a bowl of Reese's Peanut Butter mini-cups. I grab one, open the wrapper, pop it into my mouth: warm.

"Is that how I came up? Jerry and our bonus battles? He used to call year-end review 'In-Your-End.' Jerry thought we had a printing press in the basement next to the cryogenic chamber where we keep Walt Disney," he says.

"I think my brother was being blackmailed before he got murdered."

Nikolovski blinks.

"You said I only had five minutes, was he?"

"Whoever was blackmailing him only wanted his premiere passes, a couple of available screenplays, and client lists," he says.

"Who would want those kinds of things?"

"Dirty, nasty people," he says. "Hold on, I have to take this call."

Nikolovski slides on his headset, cracks his neck and swivels his chair around so I'm looking at his bald spot and a giant rip in the back of his leather chair, exposing orange foam.

"Uh huh. Uh huh. That's the Guild's position? Uh huh. Uh huh. I got it. No, I really get it. What? What?"

Nikolovski gut laughs, turns to face me, and throws off his headset.

"Are we done?"

"Jerry wrote a book about the agency. Did Lester ever mention anything to you about it?"

"Really? Am I in it?"

"No idea. I'm not sure if it even exists."

Nikolovski buzzes his assistant.

"Only one way to find out: Let's see what the coverage says."

SCHADENFREUDE: Manuscript by N/A. Submitted to Arthur Livingstone via Jerry Makos for General Consideration.

COMMENTS: If Rosemary mated with Sammy Glick, their hellish spawn might resemble something like this furious, arsenic Hollywood novel about a film student-turned-agent trainee named Cash who realizes he's delivering mail to Satan's agent. Story is determined to be spooky and amusing, suggesting the biz really is the devil's playground. Mysteriously promoted to agent, young Cash discovers his agency signed Legion months ago, and now the whole bloody building is possessed, from the sentient walls to cannibalistic, zombie janitors and cellular dwellers in their Range Rovers, to the "signers" on the second floor. Oh, and everybody in town shakes with their left hand. Cash takes on the wacky agency, saves the soul of an outside reader (until she betrays him for CAA), only to discover this shocker: Devil's been around Wilshire Boulevard forever. It was Cash's agency that had valiantly held out against the forces of the goblin for over a century. Plot usually gets thrown over for a bleak anecdote that obviously happened to someone, maybe the author, who knows? Dialogue is so "inside," the bizarre lunch conversations might as well be written in Aramaic (even for this reader). Action gets a little tedious with its endless vignettes of assassination, incest, human sacrifices at Monday morning staff meetings, and packaging fees. For our client Franklin Brauner, there's no movie here. Satanically derivative manuscript calls itself a novel when, let's be honest, this is just an axe grinding of frustration, impotence, and despair.

	EXCELLENT	GOOD	FAIR	POOR
CHARACTERS			XX	
DIALOGUE		XX		
STORY STRUCTURE		XX		
PLOT LINE			XX	

RECOMMEND_____CONSIDER_____PASS_XX_

I'm really pissed at Lester. He says he's lost his copy of Dupin's script for the second time. I can't get him on the phone. The one time he called back was to rant about "some piece of demented ass" he had the other night after dinner at Ginza Sushi-Ko, and rail against those "cock-suckers" at Fox business affairs, as if I was in on this well-known factoid. I'm looking at a pile of grey envelopes with scripts inside and realize nobody's coming up the road to get them. Maybe I wasn't worth filling out a messenger request form. I shuffle my pathetic deck of business cards, waiting to berate the assistants who haven't sent pickups, which is everyone: "He's stepped away." "She's on set." "He's wrapping up this call." "He's taking a shit." I got more hang-ups than Freud. I finally get Orly Gold on the phone and she doesn't sound too intrigued by my serial killer pitch. I'm pushing her to read the script, almost to the humiliating precipice of groveling. Supremely put-upon, Orly unconvincingly offers to send a messenger under the condition that I not place any "silly time constraints." I mention Lester Barnes made an offer to take it to MGM. Orly says, "Never look a gift whore in the mouth," and hangs up. I pour myself a triple Mandrin and spend the rest of the afternoon mesmerized by a four hour DVD of blasé European women giving head in between puffs of cigarettes, thinking about anything but what they're doing. Sound of gravel crunching under tires. I see a messenger service pulling up in front of Jerry's house. A Hispanic man with a huge mustache parks his station wagon, searches for a painted address on the curb, eye contacts me on the deck. I wave him over. Hold out an envelope containing Dupin's script, ask Super Mario who sent him, and the messenger tells me Lester Barnes. Behind him, a row of traffic has curled around my street to Canyon Drive. I notice their car doors all have decals. One guy eating a banana puts two and two together: I'm the dude. I reach for the envelope pile that has been sitting cold for weeks. Messengers line up, start pounding the door, demanding their pickup, shoving each other away like starving refugees with outstretched hands hoping to catch a humanitarian happy meal thrown their way.

"I know why all of you are here."

Every envelope gets picked up, 25 scripts in all. There can be only one explanation. Somebody read it—

VARIETY

MGM ARRESTS COP

CENTURY CITY—After a heated bidding war, the Lion has picked up "Infamous" from LAPD detective Stefani Dupin for low-six against mid-six figures. Ex-agency topper Lester Barnes will produce the project under his management-production concern. Cub scribe's deal was brokered by lit manager Josh Makos, who will also produce, and attorney Brad Blumberg of Noon, Swan, Axelman, and Packer.

☆

QUICK CHAT:
MakoShark36: Hello
JessicaWabbit: Jerry?
MakoShark36: Close
JessicaWabbit: OhMyGod!!! this is so freaky!!!
MakoShark36: What
JessicaWabbit: what's it like???
MakoShark36: Whats what like
JessicaWabbit: Hell
MakoShark36: Its me Josh, Im using Jerry's computer
JessicaWabbit: there's something called a phone you know
MakoShark36: Im aware, yes
JessicaWabbit: flake just like everyone else
MakoShark36: I'M SORRY
JessicaWabbit: what do you want
MakoShark36: did you read me in the trades
JessicaWabbit: mercy fuck
MakoShark36: it was a statement
JessicaWabbit: Tell it to a publicist, my god you've changed, scary!!!
MakoShark36: I don't need a publicist I need an assistant
JessicaWabbit: get an intern
MakoShark36: I NEED YOU
JessicaWabbit: I happen to LIKE collecting unemployment
MakoShark36: put down that bong and be a part of GURU

JessicaWabbit: sounds like cult

MakoShark36: me and Lester Barnes tomorrow both trades

JessicaWabbit: Youre going to work for Lester

MakoShark36: Partners

JessicaWabbit: Bullshit

MakoShark36: We're called Guru

JessicaWabbit: Offices where?

MakoShark36: B of A building, Beverly Hills

MakoShark36: r u there?

JessicaWabbit: 50,000, promoted after year

MakoShark36: OK, but Lester said 35

JessicaWabbit: Tell Lester two words overtime

MakoShark36: If I get you 35, will you come

JessicaWabbit: make me

MakoShark36: that's what im afraid of

JessicaWabbit: watch it you're becoming your brother

After sleeping with me at my new house at the top of the Oaks, Jessica notices the high ceilings and skylights and asks if a jolly green giant had lived here. I remember the moment I fell in love with the decrepit property, which was owned by an "extremely motivated" seller: former NBA basketball great Methuselah Dandridge, who blew out his septum, knees, and kidneys (too many Advils), traded to County Jail, where he spent a year on trumped up sodomy charges, now coaching somewhere in Greece. A suspicious fire had incinerated the pool house/media room and would have consumed the grounds were it not for a divine intervention of rain. When the building inspector told Lester's real estate lady Art Deco the cause of the fire had been electrical, Art Deco told me she said, "Maybe. If they were smoking wire." Flash of Art Deco: Funny, beautiful 40-something in a snug skirt suit, delicious New Zealand accent, who instantly revolted me after I discovered her fetish of driving while devouring McDonald's hamburgers stuffed with fries, wiping catsup from the steering wheel and licking her gruesome fingers. Art Deco opened the last black box of the day and led me past the basketballer's half court where I would never practice free throws, acknowledging, with a gasp, Methuselah's world-class infinity pool overlooking the Griffith Park observatory. Through the icy inner sanctum, footsteps clopping loudly on the hardwood floors, I remember taking in the transcendental view of Los Angeles. My low-ball offer was accepted while I was closing on Jerry's bachelor pad, which Art Deco had sold to a Hip Hop artist from Atlanta as a pied-a-terre for his Moms. Post-Infamous, Lester turned me on to his way-too-serious decorator, face pulled tight as her hairbun, who did what she could with the budget I gave her. When I requested my bookshelves be filled with titles of her selection to impress my guests, she drew the line: "I don't do libraries." After Feng Shui, Lester calls for a house-warming party. Event planners from Merv Griffin volunteer their expertise and know-how; Gavin de Becker provides security; Along Came Mary suggests a French Colonial Vietnamese vibe that promises a taste of Saigon. The exclusive invite list is controlled by Lester's office ("No Schnorrers"). As the guests start to arrive, I am told we are short on help: a few of the servants hired to serve cocktails just burned to death in the desert after fleeing a coyote van transporting illegal immigrants. I yank Jessica away from an animated conversation she's having with George Christy to tell her she'll be making her waitress debut for Guru. The walkway candles and fiery torches and dramatic lighting of Methuselah's house make the grounds resemble Asgard, high above the clouds, out of reach to the uninvited mortals below. Everybody is tripping at my party and I'm the last person to find out the Jello shots are spiked with acid—Not Good. I saw Carmen and her three girlfriends an hour ago and now they're gone. Jessica is throwing up into my pool, her hair floating in the water with guests cannonballing around her. Nazarian's fully engaged in a conversation with his Omniscience comrades, all in their early 30s, the next wave of agents waiting for any of their rising clients to open a movie at #1 so the real fucking can begin. No sign of Socrates anywhere. Hands are cupped over my eyes—

"Carmen?"

It's Dupin, looking awful, wearing a Hamburgler outfit.

"First guess, wishful thinking? Very revealing, Josh."

"Are you still L.A.P.D.?"

"I still got my gun," she says. "Don't worry Josh, we'll get him."

"You said that already, detective. Not impressed—"

Dupin sees my eyes dart to somebody behind her.

"I don't need Western Union. Get your dick wet."

Carmen, the most beautiful woman at my party, makes her way towards me, ignoring the talent agents trying to get her attention.

"How'd the audition go?"

"It turned out to be topless, so I said no."

"What about the play? All those lines!" I say.

"It's David Hare. You're coming, right?"

"Next week you said. Want a tour of the house?"

Taking my arm and sliding around her waist, Carmen nods with the vigor of a child who's just been asked if she wants ice cream.

"You're cocky. I like that in a man. True about the Jello shots?"

"You didn't take any, did you?"

Carmen holds up two fingers, crosses her eyes.

"Look at the pretty colors! Kidding! Just one."

Ascending the stairs, telling Carmen she needs more tape if I'm going to help her career, my ears pick up Socrates Wolinsky pitching some nerd from Escape Artists who can't write a check, "Exorcist meets Passenger 57." Carmen stops to appreciate the walls lined with a b/w photographic retrospective of Los Angeles: the Capitol Records building, Randy's Donuts, homeless people sleeping in cardboard boxes on Skid Row, Damian "Football" Williams poised to hurl a brick at Reginald Denny's skull at Florence and Normandie—

"You know who I aspire to be, as an actress, Josh?"

Carmen lies down on my bed. Flash of Grover fucking her and I'm jolted by my image of Carmen as tainted.

"Lena Olin."

"Suzanne Somers," she reveals.

"Don't ever tell anyone that again. Our little secret."

"So, Guru. Who'd you break in this bed with, your assistant?"

"She's so Mesopotamia."

"I'll take that as a huge yes."

I drop myself onto the bed with Carmen, slide my hand under her hair, and start kissing her neck. Carmen laughs, kisses me back. She pulls down the top of her dress, unhooks her bra, leaving on her panties.

"I don't want to complicate our relationship," she says.

Rolling around under the sheets, I get on top of her. Carmen giggles and pushes her breasts together. Welcomed aboard, I straddle her waist up to her chest, my knees in her armpits, shove a pillow under her head—

"They got the guy! Turn on the TV," shouts somebody from downstairs.

I jump off Carmen, throw on my boxer shorts, grab the remote. When I can't find the TV channel in my bedroom, I run down the hall to the media room, where hundreds of guests are watching K-CAL 9 news on the big screen. Publicity photo of my brother cuts to a reporter live from a police station:

"Tonight in Los Angeles, we have a full and complete confession from an unproduced screenwriter who claims to have murdered one of Hollywood's Top 100..."

News camera zooms in on a cardboard sign thrown onto a sidewalk. I recognize the suspect, being handcuffed on Wilshire Boulevard, surrounded by police officers. I've seen him before. I'd know that WILL SCREENWRITE FOR FOOD sign anywhere.

II

I start thinking about drinks usually around noon. I tried doing breakfast meets, but I missed so many I developed a reputation for being a flake. I like meeting the agent nitwits for lunch at Barney's Greengrass, for drinks at the Blvd of the Regent Beverly Wilshire, or the Four Seasons; I tend to socialize with studio execs by taking them to my favorite Gentleman's Club near Olympic and Sawtelle called Clams, where you can order a plate of linguini with a minimum of two non-alcoholic drinks. Jessica still can't believe I took a trio of D-girls down to the Century Lounge near LAX and paid for one of them to take a shower with a black chick. My expense account is unlimited, provided the whispers I hear about unhappy clients turn out to be accurate and lead to Guru signings that strengthen our list and make for shocking headlines. Sometimes I go to Clams for lunch, solo. Lester insists I join his dinners with executives in marketing and distribution in order to understand and appreciate the impossible, thankless, and expensive responsibility of a studio maximizing awareness through a fiendishly clever campaign, having a vote in the one-sheets, and picking the perfect release date to guarantee a #1 opening weekend for every picture involving "DQ ," Lester's longtime friend and biggest client. Every lunch, every drink, every dinner, every after-hours party is cheap pretense to the real business at hand: finding the next picture for the marquee signage on Guru's building. Every guru inside the company, especially me, wanted to be the hero who brought Lester the offer for DQ and share in the commission of a $15 million fee.

DQ was the latest of a string of big-ticket, glamorous actors who had deserted their agencies in the trades and joined Lester's Hollywood and Vine-on-Versailles. I heard about DQ's drinking and substance abuse problems, allegations about the rape of a publicist during a press junket and the costly hush payoff that forced the actor to seek a payday in a picture that tanked so royally, having a "DQ" picture now stood for "death quotient" in the minds of theatre owners. Publicly, Lester and DQ are inseparable. They lend their names to support the Ronald McDonald House, Find a Cure for MS, and Project Angel Food. They organize a Colorado river-rafting trip with studio chiefs and media company visionaries. They sign autographs at burn wards in Cedars, campaign at trendy clubs to raise awareness about the Hep-C epidemic, and host $1500 a plate fundraisers for a national missile defense shield. All smiles and no worries, Lester and DQ have everything except their next picture.

•

The guy who owed Socrates money came back from Florida with nothing. If they didn't come up with $90,000 by next week, Sundance was off, the film would never get done, and all Socrates would have to show at the end of the day, for all the blood, sweat and fear he put into the film: an IOU. Through Jessica's sister, a teacher at Hamilton High, we got half the senior class to fill up a screening room at Raleigh Studios on a Friday night. When the theatre light finally dims, the rambunctious crowd goes absolutely berserk, cheering and whistling and applauding before the crest of the very first roller coaster plunge. Props to Jessica for suggesting Lester watch the unfinished movie with a recruited audience. As the video projection begins, Jessica and I raise fists at Socrates exiting the preview of the film he'd created ("found") in the editing process. The movie tyrant Lester Barnes sits away from the riff-raff, quite regal, in the plush executive armchair back at the farthest reaches of the theatre.

On screen, over black, white letters burn in:

THE FOLLOWING IS ACTUAL FOOTAGE
TAKEN FROM A CRIME SCENE

The letters fade out, the title bleeds in:

THE GAINESVILLE EVIDENCE

Applause. Thick excitement. Jessica hits my arm playfully. I stroke her leg up to her knee and squeeze really hard, causing her to scream, which sends the theatre into a tizzy of laughter and chatter. The first thing you notice about the film is how real it seems. In a shocking series of hand-held video clips, five college students are videotaped being woken up at night, blindfolded and gagged, thrown into trunks of cars driven to an abandoned sorority house near the University of Florida, Gainesville. Then you figure out the set up once the kids are inside: Three girls and two guys recognize their abduction as a hazing ritual they all hoped wouldn't happen to them. Flashlights and hand-held digital video cameras are parceled out. No matter what they see, no matter what happens to them, if they leave the house before dawn, they will have to wait two whole semesters before they can pledge; they are not allowed to fall asleep. If they are videotaped napping, they are out. None of the undergraduates want that to happen, so they resign themselves to pulling this "all nighter-from hell," pick up their DV cameras, and make lame jokes about being in a Wes Craven movie. The second thing you notice is a running graphic "Exhibit F… Property of Gainesville PD… Evidence Room…" at the bottom of the screen, creating the effect that what you're watching is actually real. Each student explores a part of the house by themselves with their DV camera. The night explodes with rain. After a while, even I start to get bored. I look around the theatre and notice a couple of entire rows aren't watching, they're groping their dates. Those who aren't so lucky don't pay any attention to the movie; they choose to watch the couples feeling each other up instead. I am already disappointed with the movie when I catch Lester making a phone call, so captivated is he by the feature attraction. I begin to think of qualifiers to say to Lester, to apologize, to somehow make up for this fiasco. I pull my arm away from Jessica. This is not my fault. I find myself getting mad at Jessica, blaming her for making this screening such a big deal, sight unseen! Now I'm just waiting for it to end, probably got another forty-five minutes before—

The theatre awakes with such a loud eruption of terror it's like a cherry bomb going off at a funeral. On screen, a DV camera moves away from a mirror, a flashlight reflects off the glass, revealing a figure, then, a scream and the camera gets herky-jerky, as Camera Girl runs away from something, someone uninvited, and her erratic breathing only makes the moment more electrifying to watch. Her feet pound on the carpet until a floorboard gives way and, camera still recording, she falls two stories to land in the dirty, dusty old basement. Now at this point every member of the audience feels like they have taken a tumble, hurt themselves, dropped their flashlight, and found themselves in total darkness inside a basement that smells like death. "What's with the dirt?" Camera Girl asks, snatching up her flashlight when a crunching sound on the soundtrack produces audible gasps from Jessica and the couple in front of us. You definitely get the sense somebody else is down there with her in the basement. The entire movie theatre is frozen with fear. The girl on the tape is so scared she cannot breathe. I don't think I've ever in my life heard such a ghastly silence. The audience holds their breath with her. And as soon as she relaxes, my audience howls in fear! Her flashlight drops to the floor, produces a cloud of dust, goes out. Next thing you know, she's being tackled to the ground, screaming for her life. Over sounds of a young woman dying of fright, the DV camera, on its side, records her last breath. Under this, rolls: "Exhibit F… Property of Gainesville PD Evidence Room… Do Not Remove…"

Lester is still in his seat when the last student exits the screening room. His face is inscrutable, his reaction to the film, wildly unknown. An overdressed Socrates appears, expecting a check. Jessica thinks the screening went well. Lester levitates, engineers his exit between rows of red seats, unlit cigar jammed inside his jaw.

"Ready to fire up that stogie now, Lester?"

Socrates, hungry to introduce himself to his savior, steps up next to Jessica and clumsily bumps into me, just as Lester stops, regards my question and dismissively waves his Cohiba.

"Let me get back to you."

Lester's full page ads in the trades announce Guru's "temporary" address in Beverly Hills until the construction of new offices in the heart of "old Hollywood," near Hollywood & Highland, which will house Guru's permanent location of its "management-production-distribution entity." I'm looking at the extensive phone sheet Jessica has prepared and realize I don't know any of these people.

"Did you talk about promoting me with Lester?"

"I rave about you every day. How many calls this morning?"

"That's a 'No.'" says Jessica, exiting my office.

"Remind me, who's Greta Pacé?"

Back at her desk, my assistant sends me a quick-chat, which announces itself with a bass-throated burst of frog:

gruasst: You don't have to yell

guru: Who's greta pacé?

gruasst: you have lunch today

guru: don't know who she is, what does she look like, should I cancel???

gruasst: Omniscience agent, you want me to place the call, introduce you?

guru: I can introduce myself myself!

gruasst: lester from the car

guru: get off the call

gruasst: promotion you promised!!!

"Josh? Can you hear me, Josh?"

"Lester, my man!"

"That was some film you showed me the other night," says Lester.

"Are you in?"

"That was not a movie Josh. That was a phenomenon. I'm in the bathroom. I hear these kids after the show saying they're going to e-mail everybody they know, raving about that piece of crap as if it was real! I was shaking at the urinal, Josh. My entire body shook at the thought of a phenomenon for ninety fucking grand!"

"So you made the deal already?"

"Brad's the fucking best, isn't he?"

"What'd you get for it?"

"We stole it from them," says Lester.

"What's my deal?"

"Talk to Brad."

"What about my buddy Socrates?"

"Who the fuck's that?"

"The guy who edited the thing," I say.

"Oh he fucked up big time. He's lucky I didn't press charges!"

"When did all this go down? I can't believe Socrates didn't tell me!"

"Brad called, told him I was interested. This guy goes off and takes the videotapes hostage. I don't negotiate with terrorists," says Lester.

"He's not a terrorist. He's an independent filmmaker!"

"I got the Digi-Betas back in time to strike a print for Sundance, he said he wanted cash money, get this: to pay his bills, because his girlfriend ran up his cell phone charges last month."

"Lester, I hate to lose Jessica as an assistant but I really think we should—"

"Josh, I need a favor."

"Anything, say the word."

"I wouldn't ask you to do this unless—are we alone on the line?"

"We're alone Lester, now confess."

"There's this old client of mine I want you to meet. Have Jessica book a table at Barney's—Whoa! Asshole! Stop singing with your eyes closed while you're fucking driving! I'm on Rodeo, Josh."

"What's the client's name, who is he to you, what's he need?"

"Jesus your mind is processing everything these days really quickly."

"Whatever. Happy to meet him: time and a place," I say.

"His name is Franklin Brauner. He's a real auteur. Look up his credits. I'll have my office send you samples."

"Hey Lester, who's this Omniscience bitch, Greta Pacé? Who should I be talking with at that agency?"

"That's not an agency, it's a Judas factory—"

I lose him somewhere between Dayton and Beverly Drive.

I put down Brauner's script, Sky Kings. What a read. My lunch at Barney's isn't until one o'clock. Earlier, my morning began with a little Absolut Mandrin, just a little, on the rocks, now my tumbler's half full. Guess that makes me an optimist. I'm supposed to have notes for this Franklin Brauner guy, so I flip the script on my knee, dig out a pen from the sofa cushion wedge, and start writing my thoughts on the back page:

- Like the whole teenage runaway thing in S.F. Cool dialogue.

- Needs more action in the middle; got bored; what if they need to commit a crime to raise the cash to save her friend from LUTHER?

- Why does father pay him to pretend to be homeless to get back his daughter? Too vague!

- Like the Chloe-Damian scene in the "live" sex scene at the O'Farrell Theatre—fucking cool

- He's an addict, she's an addict, Damian should let Chloe leave at the end because he's a bigger drug addict than she is! That's what he's learned!

I watch the director's entire oeuvre at a double bill retrospective at the New Beverly Cinema. I fall in love with Franklin Brauner's swinging psychedelic first film, "Alamogordo." Surprisingly stylish, I'm smitten with his directing, hypnotized by the film's original, operatic score (Franklin is listed as the composer), engaged by the fearless performances, and bewitched by his camera choices. Between films, audience members on the sidewalk speak of Franklin Brauner in the past tense, as if no one believed he was still alive. All we have is the work he left behind for us to scratch our heads and wonder why the hell he'd only directed two films in his career.

I try to stay awake during the second film Franklin made fourteen years later about a TV repairman in the desert who discovers his wife is a ritualistic serial killer. According to IMDB, "Mrs. Black" got 3.8 stars—Not Good.

I'm in the shower when the phone rings. Wipe shampoo off my forehead, traipse wetly across the hallway floor, leaving puddles and foamy footprints. I grab the cordless and rather than answer it shivering in the cold air, return to the steaming hot closet, shut the glass door behind me. My voice echoes as I say hello.

"So, did you read the script last night, Josh?"

"Did you?"

It's Jessica. I'm lathering up my chest in wide circles with the shank of soap.

"I asked you first. What are you, taking a shower?"

"Am I still on for lunch?"

"Are you drunk?"

"I can't believe you just asked me that," I say.

"Well, you're on the phone inside the shower, you sound guilty, and you're slurring your words, boss."

"You are so toast," I say.

"Coverage came in. Do you care?"

"Tell me what Franklin Brauner looks like."

"Like the Devil. Wears sunglasses indoors."

"Sunglasses. Horns. Got it: What else?"

"How was the script?"

"How was the coverage?"

"He's a leper," says my assistant. "Nobody wants to work with Franklin Brauner."

"That's what the guy who used to represent him said."

"He's cursed. People die around this director. Every agent's afraid of putting their clients in his movies. I can't understand why Lester is making you meet with him."

"What do you mean, making? Lester's coming with me," I say.

"Actually, no: Lester sends regrets from the studio party plane. He's with DQ on his way to Acapulco."

"Didn't DQ used to be his chef?"

"No, he used to be a movie star," she says.

Head back, rinse scalp. Shampoo flows down the back of my calves, swirls around the drain between my feet.

"Just because the guy makes one movie every two decades doesn't mean he's a loser. Did you know he started as a painter?"

"Spare me the bio, I live in the present. I was on Lester's desk when Franklin got replaced on that movie after that Broadway actress, what's her name, asphyxiated in the makeup trailer, and that film loader fell asleep at the wheel after working nineteen hours straight—"

"Then why am I doing notes on this desperado's script?"

"Obviously, Lester wants to keep him working so he can enjoy high tea at Franklin's house in the hills," she says.

"You ever been up there?"

"Get real. Like I'm ever going to be invited anywhere."

For 20 minutes I've been driving from Barney's Greengrass to Barney's Beanery near La Cienega. I'm super pissed off at this asshole for going to the wrong place. But he's someone important to Lester so I'm the one preparing an apology for my tardiness. Inside Barney's, the malevolent director sits at the end of the bar, his face shrouded in shadow. I figure: this must be him, so I put on a big smile as I approach Franklin Brauner—

"What excuse does Lester send this time?"

His tone is so nasty I am taken aback.

"He's on the party plane to Acapulco," I say.

"With DQ," he says. "You're only forty minutes late."

"I went to the wrong Barney's. My fault," I say.

"You're the one everyone's talking about."

"Correct."

"The lit manager."

"That's what I do, not who I am. I have yet to confuse a career for a life, if that's what you're thinking."

"The way Lester raves, you're a literary messiah."

"Don't believe the hype," I wave magnanimously.

"You shouldn't feign modesty, it doesn't wear well on you. Learn to accept compliments. A simple thank you will do, every time."

"I loved Alamogordo, saw it the other night at—"

"Please. Don't be an asshole. Sit down," he says.

"Let's get a booth, we can talk about your script—"

"Excuse me! You think because you have an expense account you can rush me!"

Despite the anger flaring inside me, I take a deep breath,

try a different tack to tame this rabid, fang-baring beast:

"We can stay right here at the bar. What are you having there, Franklin? What is that, vodka?"

"I don't drink. You may order me another seltzer."

Bartender, resembling a construction worker, comes by to take our order.

"Another one for my friend here. I need a margarita, salt, Patron Silver."

"Interesting choice of tequila. You're doomed if you keep aping Lester Barnes."

"I don't ape."

"The higher the monkey climbs the pole, the more we see its ass."

"Deep, Franklin."

The director laughs, hacking into a body-racking coughing spasm.

"The Israelis (cough! cough!) pulled out today."

"Out of what, the West Bank?"

"Sky Kings."

"Lester said you had diamond merchants financing the film?"

"I had a cast, a crew (cough! cough!), a start date and a million dollars. Last minute: one guy drops out, Israeli partner gets nervous, needs to talk to his wife, they all get Catholic, everybody pulls out," he says.

"Franklin, that's heartbreaking."

"Now I have to tell the crew, my actors, 'Terribly sorry you turned down jobs to make my movie, but the (cough! cough!) money fell out.' Agents, I'm sure, will trash my name in staff meetings so I'll never, ever, get a soul on the phone, or a set, for that matter, if I ever get (cough! cough!) off the ground."

I sip my margarita: too strong, my stomach instantly revolts.

"Look at it this way: now you're available," I say.

Inside his jacket pocket, Franklin Brauner shows me a gleaming pistol.

"I love the line in Taxi Driver where Marty asks DeNiro 'Did you ever see what a .44 magnum can do to a woman's pussy? Now that you should see—'"

"Franklin, put that thing away!"

"Or what (cough! cough!), they'll toss me in jail? I'm already in the ninth circle! (cough! cough!) You try living there."

"That can't be good. Lung cancer?"

"My allergies are killing me. I told Lester: put me up for an assignment, that Tom B. Raider executive (cough! cough!) stole my take."

"Sounds like you didn't get the job."

"Well, fucking pay me for the fax I sent that made them half a billion dollars!"

"This sense of entitlement doesn't wear well on you."

I tell Franklin Brauner about the successful outcome of Infamous, written by a detective on my brother's case, which remains unsolved. He showed absolutely no interest about the bidding war, the name of the exec on the project, or the studio development process.

"Balzac said, 'Behind every fortune is a crime.'"

"What's your theory, Franklin?"

"I think you're nobody in this town 'til everybody thinks you're a bastard."

"Does that go double for you?"

"No, every bastard in this town thinks I'm a nobody," he says.

"Who do you think killed Jerry?"

"Agents: With 'em, without 'em, can't live."

"Did you know my brother?"

"Who do you think found the Israelis?"

Jessica and I have one rule: no fucking at the office. Whenever someone wants something from me, generally I eat for free. If it's someone who has something I need, I take the cheque. Franklin is using me for my expense account. I've never once seen him take out his wallet, even when we were out with his friend Barbet Schroeder at the Derby with those Algerian composers from Paris. I know he's a client, but I draw the line at buying groceries. I complain to Lester, who can't be bothered with Franklin Brauner tossing toilet paper, baguettes and veal shanks into my cart at Rock n' Roll Ralphs when DQ is turning down studio offers, beating up producers at restaurants, pleading in court, landing on every cover of the tabloids.

Gruasst: Bryan from McG's office

Guru: tell him set visit

Guru: you going to MANZANAR?

Gruasst: none of yer beeswax

Guru: r u mad at me?

Gruasst: Kaylee from warners

Guru: tell her im in a meeting with DQ

Gruasst: are you taking anybody?

Guru: roll calls from the car

Gruasst: Tanya from Cinema Shares regarding Gainesville, Lorenzo on the bottom, some guy from Bellerophon, Carmen on top

Guru: I'll take Carmen

Gruasst: love me fuck me promote me you dick

Guru: that's a lester call

Gruasst: Did you hear from Oliver re: Infamous

Guru: Stone passed
Gruasst: I'm rooting for Franklin Brauner
Guru: please take that guy off call sheet
Gruasst: did you talk to Lester about Sundance?
Guru: if you want to go he said your dime
Gruasst: what a hebe
Guru: watch it
Gruasst: fuck him, fuck DQ, fuck this whole place
Guru: don't hold anything back Jessica, tell me how you really feel

I'm in the Chrysler drunk as shit after 14 lychee martinis with some Korean movie producer who's got remake rights to the #3 all-time box office champ in the Philippines when Dupin calls, sniffling in my ear like she's been crying/doing coke for days—

"I met this client who I think would be a great choice to direct Infamous."

"Josh, I'm no longer on that project."

"I thought you had one more pass! How many steps do you have left?"

"Oh, I've been through all the steps: Despair, Anger, Acceptance—"

"I got you a meeting with Gwartz at Paramount."

"I know him! He wanted me to do the rewrite on Philosophical Crisis!"

"No, he's the exec who went with some friend of Lester's who pitched the morning of your meeting: I heard it was his to lose."

"Thanks for telling me. I would've appreciated knowing that."

"Not really. If I'd told you what Lester told me before your meeting, you'd be all pissed off at Gwartz instead of giving him love at the mention of his name!"

"What's bothering you, Josh?"

"Nothing! I'm just running late."

"No, there's something terribly wrong in your voice, I can hear it, something's wrong, you're angry with me."

"I think you care more about time-traveling killers than real ones," I finally say what's been on my mind since MGM bought her script.

"That's not fair! I've been busy addressing everybody's notes. Infamous got put into turnaround this morning, Josh. They gave Lester a short window to set it up someplace else, but I'm not optimistic. I bet all those people who didn't get the script hate you now."

"W-Who hates me?"

"What if I said Donna D'Amato at New Line called you narrow?"

"Oh c'mon, she's only in the film business by virtue of her uterus."

"Just because she had Chip's baby doesn't mean she doesn't have great taste! God, you sound just like Lester: he's the reason I can't meet my fans at Disney because 'low-six figures' means—"

"I can't hear you."

I click off my cell as I pull up to the Mink Slide, surrounded by military grade barbed wire, noticing an armed "guard" atop a constructed wooden "MANZANAR" lookout tower atop the roof. On the sidewalk elderly wrinkled Japanese women are washing clothes by hand in large aluminum tubs of soapy water. I push my way into the bar, where Franklin is engrossed in conversation with a group of E.R. nurses from Good Sam.

Franklin refuses to discuss Infamous with me until Lester has given him the script to direct. I don't have the heart to tell him we're still waiting on Terry Gilliam. So I listen to the auteur pine for alternate sources of financing for Sky Kings, which I've decided is a hard sell after I slipped it to a few nitwits (my cosmos dimmed every time I brought it up in conversation), or go over impossible casting wish-lists for his proposed adaptation of Nabokov's Pale Fire. Whatever caché Franklin Brauner may have brought to Guru's client list, Lester only gave me this high-maintenance client so he could zero in on the swizzle stick's next release, DQ's "Welcome to Manzanar," a courtroom drama inside a Japanese internment camp nobody has seen because no advance screenings were scheduled—Not Good.

"I see DQ doing Infamous, don't you?"

"Lester will never go for it," I say.

"He will after he reads my polish," says Franklin.

"What about Ashley Judd as the bounty hunter from the future?"

"I only need DQ. That role is a star-maker, not for a star to make."

"I can't get my head around DQ playing a serial killer."

"Deep down, they all want to go dark. They're sick to death of saving the world," says Franklin.

"How much work do you need to do on the script?"

"Couple of weeks. The whole thing needs noodling, a fresh coat of paint, a fluff and a tuck. I have to write a character DQ can't refuse. He's got to be really out there. I know what I'd want to see when I go see this movie."

"Franklin, I want to make a movie everyone will want to see."

"I know exactly what people want! I know exactly what needs to be done to this script. I know exactly (cough! cough!) how to make it."

"Great, all I have to do is cut DQ's price and find you 30 million," I say.

"Just get me in a room with DQ. Lester has his turnaround so we can make this script the way it should be made."

"You are out there, Franklin."

"I am out there, Josh. I have to make this script. I believe the gods have a reason for bringing you and this script into my life. At the end of this, I'll know what everything is supposed to mean. I'm putting aside Sky Kings (cough! cough!), we'll make it later. I'll get Larry McConkey to hold our steadicam, find some real actors, shoot it on HD so we can wash the stain off, like Gus did after Good Will Hunting. Lester only thinks about the deal. Your brother, on the other hand, was paid to think about movies."

"I'm not my brother, Franklin. Have to tell you that right now," I say.

"You think I don't know making movies is difficult? You child! You have no clue what disappointment means. You've never had your spleen yanked out of your body by ten executives at Columbia Pictures! You've never known betrayal until you've been stabbed in the front! Outside the Ivy! By your wife! How could I possibly have any expectations for any of this to actually happen?"

"You're right, Franklin, you're right. There's a fucking boatload I don't know about this business, but you know what? It doesn't matter! Because the perception is: I know something, and I'm doing a banner job managing my perception. I can keep winging it so long as the nitwits believe I get the joke."

"If it turns out you never knew what you were talking about, if you are exposed, then every right decision you made was a fluke, and you will find yourself miserably alone," he says.

"Is that how everybody in this business ends up?"

"Josh: They're called producers."

Grabbing a sake martini off a tray, enjoying the "detention" theme while chewing inside-out California rolls, I realize everyone is shaking their heads in total shame, denying Christ countless times that they had anything to do with the decision to green-light the movie. I pay respect to the DJ Rickie Rick, writer of Amsterdamned, a script I like about a band of Belgian video store clerks and their "Oceans 11-on-water." Lester Barnes leaves a table of CAA agents. I make my move—

"We have to talk."

"Good luck," he says.

"What's that, Lester?"

"That's what the marketing guy said to me tonight, only he said it like, 'Good Ruck!' Did I tell you DQ wants to be Infamous when he grows up?"

"DQ wants to play the time-traveler? We have to put him in a room with Franklin."

"Franklin Brauner? You been up to his house?"

"Not for high tea," I say.

"The view is just unbelievable. I thought he was doing Sky Kings on HD, or the Nabokov thing with Mickey Rourke?"

"That's not gonna pop in my lifetime. It's just as hard to make a movie digitally as it is going about doing it on film. I told Franklin he could rewrite it."

"Has he told you his ideas?"

"And they're absolutely brilliant. Franklin Brauner is the choice," I say.

"Talk to Brad."

"I already did."

"And?"

"We're calling it a polish, Writer's Guild minimum, he's the director until we tell him he's not the director."

"I need to go home, pack for Park City," says Lester.

"Did I hear you sign off on everything I just told you?"

"One day, you'll appreciate the joy of having a son, Josh."

"Big whatever, Lester. I'll tell Franklin he can commence."

Clutching his cigar, Lester slides away from me to accept a kiss on the cheek from Jessica, who has arrived with Nazarian from Omniscience. She whispers something very important into his ear for a very long time.

"What did you say to Lester?"

"Nothing important, boss. You know Bramley," she introduces us.

"DJ slip you the latest draft of Amsterdamned?"

"Yup," I lie, deciding to test Nazarian.

"I think the rewrite took it two steps back," he says.

"And you sold something when?"

"Last week, Wesley Strick pitch. 5 against 1.8," he says.

"Those guys would buy anything, they're worse than Morgan Creek. We should get together for some face-time," I say.

"Or maybe," he slimes me, "we'll just have drinks."

•

Franklin is smiling like I've never seen him so happy: I just told him about DQ. His handsome face turns craggy when he grins, revealing unimaginable stress lines. Above our heads blasts Giorgio Moroder's Maniac when the Bug, all excited, suddenly pulls me away—

"I got Harry Hamlin to do a cameo!"

I look over and Franklin is no longer at the bar. He's on the dance floor, letting it all hang out with the nurses. I wave, get a nod from Franklin between coughs.

"Who's the Travolta?"

"That's my client Franklin Brauner. I got him a job directing a DQ movie."

"How come you don't give me a DQ movie? You treat me like I'm some kind of fucking asshole," the Bug screams.

"He's got other projects! You want stars? They're all going to want to act in Franklin's next film! I want him to meet you."

"When he's done dancing, come to my table for some Dom."

Franklin could care less about meeting the Bug. Still coughing profusely, I pull him away from his harem and I notice Siobhan is not working behind the bar. Introductions are made at the Bug's booth.

"Let me give you a card, free dry cleaning for a month," says the Bug.

"That's quite all right. You don't have to do that," says Franklin, fingering the sweaty flute but he doesn't raise the bubbly to his lips.

"So you got DQ for your movie," says the Bug.

"Deal hasn't closed yet," says the director.

"Who's financing?"

The director shrugs, enigmatic: We have DQ.

"DQ is expensive. What's the budget? You're gonna wanna shoot in Bulgaria. I got my own production company. You know why I call it Bellerophon?"

Franklin's eyes dart over to mine: Save me.

"Hollywood is like a Chimera, this fire-breathing beast with the body of a goat, the head of a lion, and serpent's tail! Bellerophon was this Greek hero—"

"I'm familiar with the myth," says Franklin.

"Bellerophon was famous for slaying the Chimera—"

"On the winged horse Pegasus. Bellerophon (cough!

cough!) also made his name conquering the Amazons," says Franklin.

"Not what he's known for," argues the Bug.

"Bellerophon was just like his old man, Sisyphus. You remember Sisyphus, he's the one who fed the Gods human flesh. Bellerophon became so full of himself, so offensively presumptuous, he flew up to Mount Olympus, and the immortals caused his winged horse to rear and fling Bellerophon ingloriously to earth. He spent the rest of his life crippled, blind, and avoided. Pegasus got turned into Alpo."

My eyes wander and settle on Socrates at the bar, downing a vodka cran, looking heavier, meaner than I last saw him. When Socrates heads for the exit, I leave the table to go talk to him outside—

"You're quite the storyteller, Franklin. One hell of a director! I hope one day you'll pay Bellerophon a visit," says the Bug.

"Oh, I will," Franklin leans in, "and I'll say, light starch."

As I push open the heavy door of the Mink Slide, Socrates Wolinsky is lying in wait for me on the sidewalk.

"If this is about Carmen, you can have her, man. Her boyfriend's on the warpath."

"Socrates, listen to me. You're the only guy who's been a friend—"

"Friends? You think we're friends?"

"Since Jerry got killed. I'm sorry about Lester—"

"I took the money," he says.

"What money—"

"That guy Brad told me what the deal is, so save your tears."

"What money?"

"I'm in on the hype. My name's gonna be nowhere so

all of you can pretend Gainesville is real."

"Socrates, I had no idea."

"Yeah, you did. I took the fucking money. Everybody's taking an associopath credit, except you and Big Lester."

"Socrates: if it's supposed to be 'found footage,' how can you be at the screening? Sort of destroys the purpose, doesn't it?"

"Whatever, Sammy . You were going to drive me to Park City, remember?"

"Let me make things right. You want representation? I'll get you an agent."

"I had an agent—your brother—he was useless!"

"If it wasn't for Jerry, we wouldn't even be having this conversation."

"Fuck that guy! We shouldn't be having this conversation! We should be driving together to Sundance!"

Headlights from Sunset suddenly blind us. We shield our eyes to find a blue Mazda RX-7 crossing the double lines of the road towards the club.

"That's Grover's car," says Socrates.

"It is Grover!"

"He's not slowing down either."

"Jesus Christ, he's gonna jump the curb, get out—"

THE Hollywood *REPORTER*

Police Speculate Mink Slide Atrocity Result of 3 Strikes Law

SILVER LAKE—The ex-parolee who drove his car into industry hangout The Mink Slide, killing seven people, was facing life in prison, police said. According to witnesses, Grover Murray, 32, survived the explosive crash, then shattered a beer bottle to cut his own throat. Tens of bar patrons were injured. Among the dead were: Tawny Bryce and Michael Rabolli, a pair of well-liked Fox drama development execs who came up through the UTA ranks together; Good Morning L.A.'s Bumble Kinney, and the CAA

See *ATROCITY* on page 45

ATROCITY

Continued from page 1—

assistant Molly Nix. Shaken survivors included Martin Landau, Clive Owen, Guru's Josh Makos and director Franklin Brauner, who shared credit for saving the lives of three E.R. nurses. Brauner, repped by Guru and attorney Brad Blumberg, previously directed cult classics "Mrs. Black" and "Alamogordo" told HR he is working on a "very top secret" Lester Barnes project. Calls to Guru were not returned.

I'm clinking as I step onto the warm tarmac, towards the sleek jet that conjures up for me a sensation of what being on the Concorde must be like. Lester Barnes is gesticulating forcefully to nobody in particular. Thanks to the Malibu getaway and Ligeia, his personal trainer, Lester looks like God with a headset—

"Okay, okay, okay: You want to hear it? I fucked you! There, I said it. Feel better? I fucked you Roger! It's my project now! Are you still coming by the house for dinner next Sunday? Good, bring the kids."

I'm self-conscious about the clinking sounds coming from my carry-on bag, so I pick up the shoulder bag with both hands and carry it towards a step ladder where the flight attendant is waiting to flash a perfectly-timed welcoming smile. I panic about the clothes I packed for the festival. If it snows, I could buy a souvenir turtleneck or just stay indoors the whole time and drink. The thought of dry state Utah so frightened me I packed three quarts of Absolut Mandrin from the Beverage Warehouse along with the outfit I would wear for the premiere of Gainesville. I wave good morning at Lester, who snubs me with a curt flick of his head. Top of the morning to you, too. The flight attendant introduces herself as "Marlena" and moves to collect my bag from me. Thrown by Lester's gnarly mood, I am absent with the hand-off, which Marlena fumbles, surprised by the sudden weight of three bottles of Mandrin. Her face shows alarm as both of us lunge for the falling bag, two outfielders running for the same line drive and our foreheads collide.

Inside the Hawker Siddeley business jet, I plop down in a leather seat with a stack of today's trades, printed out e-mails, assorted envelopes and my Blackberry. Earlier, on the way to the airport, I heard Jessica say to me for the last time, "Here are your trades." She'd even highlighted the headlines of the articles I should read in pink—

"Et tu, Jessica," I said.

"I made up my mind about something last night, Josh."

"Not now Jessica!"

"When you get back, I don't think it's a good idea that we fuck anymore."

"What is this? Did Bramley get to you?"

"They offered me a coordinator position in their IFD division," she said.

"Jessica, am I supposed to believe you woke up in the middle of the night and decided you wanted to get into acquisitions for Omniscience?"

"I'm just saying we shouldn't be having sex anymore, okay? I'm no longer cool with it. There's really nothing in it for me I've decided," she said.

"Fine. You want to leave, leave! But I want two weeks from you. Not until you've trained your replacement—"

"I'm leaving today."

"You're going to Omniscience?"

"No, Park City. To hype your movie."

"Wait, wait: You're leaving my office in the hands of some floater before we even get the Amsterdamned offer? You can't!"

"Fox passed. Her assistant read the script this morning on the treadmill."

"Not Good, Jessica. OK, moving on: Tell me we got the coverage of that book Franklin wants to adapt," I said.

"The Nabokov thing?"

"Yes, the Nabokov coverage. Where the hell is it?"

"You got a message from Cedars-Sinai hospital: The reader tried to kill himself. Couldn't do the coverage, said it drove him insane."

"Don't leave me. Jessica please—"

"You never fought for me, Josh. You never went in to ask for my raise after Brad totally lied to my face. You never closed the door in Lester's office and said, 'We really should promote Jessica or we're going to lose her,' did you?"

"You're right. You're absolutely right," I said.

"I think you like keeping your friends down. Don't worry, I'll still be in your life: You just can't fuck me or watch me finish myself off," she said.

"Can we at least roll calls from the car?"

Fuck, I'm going to miss her. I order vodka, rocks from Marlena, who's still rubbing her bump from our collision. I pass through the back of the cabin, arrive at the lavatory, which is occupied, when I make eye-contact oh-so-briefly with a yawning blonde who's impossibly gorgeous at this early hour, not a fleck of makeup on her face, cleavage showing under her cashmere overcoat.

"You look comfy. Only thing missing from this photo is a fireplace," I say.

"Mmmm. We should have one on the plane back."

"Ask Lester. They call me Josh, looks like we're on the same flight."

"Are you his assistant?"

"Actually, I'm Lester's partner."

"Ooops! Let me pull my ass out of my mouth. I'm Noelle. Wait. I know you from somewhere. Help me out here," she says.

Sound of toilet flushing.

"You're not the guy from Deena's wedding, are you?"

The door latch opens. "DQ" steps out, three days of

facial hair, wearing a grubby red and black checkered lumberjack shirt pulled over designer jeans. Paul Bunyan at $15 million a picture.

"Have you met Josh?"

I hold out my hand. DQ gestures at the bathroom he just exited, smiles at me. I withdraw the handshake. Slowly. We both crack up.

"I've heard all about you. Lester says you're like a son," says DQ.

"Is that why he beats the shit out of me?"

"Got any grin?"

"I don't, I'm sorry—"

Conversation instantly over, I have nothing to offer DQ, who takes his seat next to Noelle. They are sweet with each other. They do this thing with their noses, kissing like Eskimos, counting and smacking their lips on the "10" count. I can't believe she's his publicist. I take my seat up front, shove my hand into the pile of scripts, manila envelopes, Industry screening invites, and gash my finger with a nasty paper cut. Variety headline shouts: "WILD 'SWAMP' THING MAKES HEARTS SING!" Hollywood Reporter: "NO WELCOME FOR MANZANAR." DQ's movie over the weekend grossed a disappointing 6.7, spanked by some animated E.T. knockoff about a Cajun boy and his CGI swamp thing, voiced by Shaq, which stunned the industry with a record haul of 46.4 million over three days. The heads of the top three distribution departments of the studios accepted the numbers, pointed fingers, or took all the credit, respectively. In both articles, Lester, speaking for his client DQ, is quoted bashing the release's handling, blaming the studio's sudden, irrational decision to shift the film's original release date to late January, and crucifying the guy who came up with the gloomy poster. I shared Lester's anger at the way the movie was handled. I still don't get how the studio makes these decisions, or why, but I was angry about the shrapnel. By now, I'd been to enough premieres to know when movies bomb at the box office, everyone involved has a dead baby on their hands. You don't even ever bring it up: It's like there's this little coffin in the room that nobody wants to talk about. Trades should have read: "WE WUZ ROBBED!" "DQ: 'MANZANAR' NO DEAD BABY!" I look up from the B.O. report and spill my drink when the agent Bramley Nazarian boards the plane with some Vietnamese chick, followed by Lester, who offers me a high-five. I slap his hand, hard. Lester loves it, moves to be with his client and Noelle, who greets Lester with a sweet, lingering kiss on the lips. Lester feigns a heart attack.

"Hey, Crash," says Nazarian, needling me about Amsterdamned's demise.

"I'm still alive. A few producers are debating if they'll use discretionary."

I know how desperate that sounds.

"Sounds promising," says Nazarian.

Smug fuck. Then I remember he's our agent. He works for me.

"Who's the Casualties of War chick?"

"Lester's manicurist. I'm gonna need her the next two weeks. IFD's selling like, ten films at the festival," says Nazarian.

"Gainesville, baby. It's all about Gainesville."

"All that hand-held stuff made me sick. I thought it was as boring as a dog's ass. You suckered Lester good with that stacked audience," says Nazarian.

"Sucker nothing, the kids went nuts," I say.

"Exactly my point. How's it going to play at midnight in a theatre packed with acquisitions people, all in their

30s? Hate to break it to you Josh, but they're exhausted, all they want to do is go to bed. They don't care about your over-hyped, slapped together, wanna-be snuff film!"

"Whatever. Go back to your Kurt Wimmer script."

Angela, the other, lovelier stewardess, arrives with my drink. Lester's manicurist sits next to Nazarian, concentrating on filling in the character of Mowgli with a maroon Crayon inside her Disneyland coloring book. Marlena and Angela take their seats, prepare for takeoff.

I'm on my third vodka.

"No way would I," says DQ.

"I would," votes Nazarian.

"You would not," DQ cringes, "Jesus! Mary and Joseph."

"Lester, settle this," says Nazarian.

"What are you guys talking about?"

"Debating Martha Coolidge ," spakes Lester, who never looks up from the manicure station set up for him in the back of the plane.

"Martha Coolidge?"

Vietnamese chick is doing Lester's feet with a pumice stone.

"That's it, come on," says Lester. "Scrape my sole."

Vietnamese chick has a sense of humor. She covers her smiling face with a hand, the one holding the rock. Lester looks up, turns to me.

"The question is: would you fuck Martha Coolidge?"

"I'd fuck her," I say.

Pull the pin, wait.

"But I wouldn't hire her!"

Everybody, and the manicurist is the loudest, cracks up. I find the Leonard Maltin Film & Video guide Jessica snuck in my script pile as a farewell in-joke.

"Human life is but a series of footnotes," Vietnamese manicurist says, "to a vast, obscure, unfinished masterpiece."

"Who said that?" asks Lester. "That's the most beautiful thing I've ever heard. Did your mother tell you that when you were little?"

Vietnamese manicurist shrugs, keeps filing his toenails. "I heard somebody earlier talking about Nabokov."

"That was Nabokov? You're far too intelligent to be working on your knees for a living! Josh, I just hired a new reader! Give her a script, will you? I don't want you to do coverage. I want you to be able to give me a verbal in front of people. Do we have a brilliant script on board? Is anyone reading a brilliant script?"

Noelle and DQ shoot their hands up, cuddling under a blanket, reading a screenplay together. They wait until the other has finished the page before turning to the next.

"See their lips, they're moving at the same time," whispers Lester.

"It's like they're reading the Yellow Pages, that thing."

"They don't wait for coverage. Need a refill there, Josh?"

"Am I in an open coffin, Bramley?"

"Guys: Knock it off," Lester warns us, firmly.

"Am I being lowered into the ground or something? Is that why you're shoveling dirt in my face in front of everybody?"

"Shrieking. Hello. Whatever."

"Guys! Guys! Somebody call David Fincher!" Lester gets between us.

"Why don't you two fuck and get it over with?" Vietnamese manicurist napalms us.

"Why don't you go back to Saigon?" punches Nazarian.

"I'm from Cambodia, dickhead."

"Bitch, I'm Armenian, so don't go crying to me about genocide!"

I discover an unfamiliar bulky overwritten screenplay atop the paper-and-brass mountain of material, centered and titled, "Dark Matter." Inside the script, I find a folded envelope marked urgent, personal and confidential, in calligraphic writing that could only be Franklin's. Jessica included the pleated envelope because it also served as Franklin's cover letter: I am late with the script. I know I am fired. So, I fire myself! Gone to Persia, F. Underneath his initial, Franklin drew a gauche doodle of the number 9 standing and fucking the number 6, who's doing a headstand. I consider picking up and reading the polymath's adaptation but then I think about what Pale Fire did to the last guy and throw it back into the pond like a snakehead.

"What do you got there, are those scripts?"

"You know what happens to girls who are nosy, Noelle?"

I pull Franklin Brauner's script from the top of the pile.

"They get to read gold!"

"Don't fuck with me, really?"

Noelle is thrilled to be a collaborator.

"Dark Matter, very cool title. What's going on with this?"

"It's an adaptation by an important director of a very famous book by Nabokov. You do know who Nabokov is, right?"

"I read the Iliad," Noelle huffs, and takes to her seat.

Like everyone else in Park City, I am underdressed. I stop to rest, catch my breath but really I'm fighting fucking severe panic disorder, dependent on a cane after I slipped on the ice outside our condo and twisted my ankle. According to the yellow and orange flyers taped around every street sign, lamp post, and parking meter on Main Street, a terrible crime has recently been committed. Flyers ask: HAVE YOU SEEN ME? I notice a hypothermia-ridden homeless man holding out a plastic Big Gulp with a taped plea: "Not a Filmmaker. Please Help." I take pity. Throw in a buck.

"Here you go, old man. Use it to buy yourself an HD camera."

"Thanks. You have a film in competition?" He's hip.

"I don't know anything about that, have a good day."

"Every day above ground is a good day."

He laughs, thanks me, and grabs my wrist. His fingers are icy.

"Get off me, Tonto! I gave you a dollar!"

The Native American lets go my wrist, says he is a medicine man, and wants to give me an Indian name. The old shaman starts to sing, low in the throat. For a good minute I indulge this silly religious shenanigan.

"You giving me a name or not?"

"You choose the dance, but you will only dance a short while."

I bolt from the chief. Lester, DQ, and Noelle wave their arms at me to keep up with them. I look back at the chief and where he once stood shaking a cup of coins there's only a wooden statue outside a cigar store. I tilt up my forehead to feel the sun. My cane slips. I fall, re-injuring my ankle. I see the movie star, Lester, and Noelle climbing the front steps to claim our reservation at Grappa. I'm on my ass, snowflakes falling into my eyes, making me blink when a greasy looking teenager in a green parka hands me a bright orange flyer: HAVE YOU SEEN ME? For more information about the case, the flyer directs the public to the Egyptian Theatre at midnight tonight so they can EXAMINE THE EVIDENCE for themselves. I spit out dirty snow, look across the street, notice the teams of actors Lester hired to hand out photos of the Gainesville kids and ask pedestrians if they've seen their friends? One of the volunteers on the street team is taking the bereavement act way too far: she's crying, dangerously underdressed, tip of her nose is frostbitten. It's Jessica, shivering, lips blue, screaming my name with surprise—

"Josh! Wait up, Josh!"

I raise my cane to engineer my snub as I climb the steps to Grappa, where I intend to order the highly recommended starter of mango calamari salad, followed by the special entrée of seared duck breast and wonton cone with fried rice and Sichuan peppers. Cappuccino sounds good, too, if I have enough room to order the mixed berry cobbler for dessert.

The lights slowly dim inside the Egyptian. Pure TNT. A few "Yeahs!" shatter the stillness. The hype on this screening is already suffocating. I overhear Lester boasting to DQ how I got propositioned last week in a men's room stall at The Mink Slide, turning down a bullshit $25,000 bribe from some acquisition exec's assistant looking for a bootleg DVD of Gainesville. Earlier,

Nazarian warned Lester about the possibility of a Sundance backlash: too much saturation before a screening could spell death and lead to bad buzz: Guess what? The movie's unwatchable! Lester reminded Nazarian if he wanted Roger Ebert, he could call him on his cell. There is a genuine scream. Someone goes, "Holy Shit! Are you okay?" The lights come up. Crowd groans: you get the feeling something's broken and the screening may get cancelled. Lester snaps his fingers. Nazarian goes to find out what's wrong in the projection booth. The girl who screamed is holding the top of her head with both hands and looking up at the ceiling, old and starting to crumble. Nazarian returns to his Gainesville platoon, assures us we're fine now, flips the bird to somebody he sees in the crowd. Lester and DQ and Noelle head for the exit. The lights go out as the film projector beams a bridge of light across the canyon of antsy acquisition executives. Nazarian whispers a joke to the manicurist, who covers her smile, all buddy-buddy with the agent, but would I not put a knife under my pillow if I ever went to bed with this climber?

On screen, over black, white letters burn:

LESTER BARNES PRESENTS

The letters fade out.

THE FOLLOWING IS ACTUAL FOOTAGE
TAKEN FROM A CRIME SCENE

The title bleeds in:

THE GAINESVILLE EVIDENCE

I wake up in a strange bed, my head surrounded by fluffy pillows. I'm not just hung over, feels like I got gout. I slide out from under the lead layer of comforters and sheets and I can't stand on my feet. I remember shredding my ankle on the sidewalk, I remember Jessica freezing to death outside Grappa, I remember what I had for dinner, I remember what had to be the single worst screening ever in U.S. film festival history. I have no clue how I ended up here, in my own room, in this monster bed, breathing the heated air of Lester's inestimable rental where I can see skiers on the mountain already, and the crush of the breakfast movie line forming outside the Egyptian, sipping Starbucks, gabbing on cell phones, wearing their laminated passes. I remember taking a "karaoke cab" to a condo party somewhere in Deer Valley with a bunch of people from the screening, and singing the words to Pat Benatar's "Hit Me With Your Best Shot." Otis Day and the Knights were playing in the living room of a condo packed with hundreds of people peeling off their coats and sweaters, steam coming off the top of their heads. I think a distributor named "Edgar" was there last night. I think I may have called him a mohel. I remember running into some toddler in the kitchen with a connection to Edgar who felt this awkward need to remind me of when and how we had first met as I was performing a vodka search inside the refrigerator. I only found Absolut Peppar, which always upsets my stomach, but I was loyal to my brand. I think I slighted the nephew with, "Put it in writing, okay? I'm off-duty." Several messages on my cell phone from

Jessica, calling to offer me anything I need while I'm here; says she's crossing her fingers for "Edgar." I skip over her rambling to messages from acquaintances, phonies, nitwits, skipping until I recognize the voice of Franklin. He'd found a few typos and (cough! cough!) wanted to hear my thoughts on the material. I'll call the auteur when I get back. His Nabokov script is probably still on the floor of the lavatory. The movie star couldn't finish Dark Matter so why should I even bother? I don't want Franklin to send me another copy. I'm sick of reading scripts. I want grin.

I smell like an orange. I'm wearing three layers of damp, unclean long-sleeved shirts soaked with Mandrin vodka. If I want to get drunk today walking around Main Street, all I have to do is suck on my arm. Somehow, during the flight, the bottles of Absolut shattered. The first layer of shirt, which is dry, feels like bark against my nipples. I already cannot deal with maddening razor sharp crystals embedded everywhere in my clothes. Incredibly, there was a sole survivor. Next I attempt with solemn concentration a ship-to-ship transfer of precious cargo, spilling Mandrin into Jerry's colorful deer skin bodabag, the one with dangling turquoise beads from a peace pipe. The bodabag came from Paul Newman, who Jerry always thought was better in that movie anyway. As I limp through the elegant condominium, my cane making imprints on the white carpet, I take in other people's bedrooms and their unmade beds; passing through the kitchen, egg flecked dishes on the table, stink of bacon. I borrow someone's jacket from a closet, take a black knit cap that says "EXHIBIT F… THE GAINESVILLE EVIDENCE…" slide it over my head, tuck in loose bangs of hair sticking out. I need to get my festival pass when I collide with a supermodel who introduces herself as "Tess" while she grabs a six pack of Fresca out of a cooler. I find out she's a paralegal with "Mr. Blumberg" and discover everybody I came here with is dressed and waiting by the fax machines. I'm the last one up. I feel like a loser.

"Well, don't you look a sight," says Noelle.

"Where's DQ?"

"In the bathroom with a script. I think he's forgotten where he is."

"Must be a pretty good script," I say.

Negotiating on the phone, waving a fax through the air, Brad Blumberg snaps his fingers, two shotgun blasts: Shut Up. I'm immediately chastised and fury bubbles inside me. Phone connection gets lost, everyone hangs up, waits for the ring. The room relaxes. Lester, wearing an argyle sweater over jeans and snakeskin cowboy boots, makes a fallow gesture in my general direction.

"A word with you, Josh? In private."

We are standing in the hallway outside the bedroom as Lester closes the door, telling the room to retrieve him when the distributor calls back.

"Did you make any assurances to Edgar at Victor Draish's condo?"

"I may have called him a mohel," I say.

"Is that a compliment? What else do you think you said?"

"I may have told someone to put it in writing. Did someone say I did?"

"Edgar wants you dead," warns Lester. "He says you sold him the film."

"I never said anything to Edgar!"

"Josh, today might be the last day we spend in Park City. Any movie you want, this will get you in, just walk past the lines."

I bow my head to accept Lester draping his laminated all-access pass around my neck like a medal.

"You're going to scope out the town today, hand over your business cards to all the hot young fresh talent. Pay attention to writer-directors. Forget the unknown actors in these films. Fuck them if you can. But: You do not fuck and then ignore an auteur in this business. This will boomerang you in the ass five years from now when that guy has a monster hit on his hands."

"Lester: I didn't say anything."

"We only get one shot at this life, Josh. Try to have as many different experiences as you can today. Fall in love. Do something once that scares you. Hug a volunteer. Don't dismiss the world cinema section, see lots of shorts, visit house of docs, hang out and listen to the media arts panels. I want a full report when you get back, what is that smell?"

Lester leans in to sniff, recoils.

"Is that Mandrin you're wearing?!"

I don't look to see who is calling me out on Main Street. I'm still paranoid about being identified to Edgar. I pop another Vicodin. I'm wasted, my legs give out, and I topple down, hit my chin on the snowy sidewalk. Taste of blood in my mouth. Sold the film to Edgar? What the fuck happened? Did I? Wait a minute. Wait a minute. Wait a minute! We sold the film! I see an acquisition exec talking into his Motorola, singling me out on the street like a pod person from that Invasion of the Body Snatchers movie. People are staring at me as I walk gingerly past the line at the Egyptian Theatre. Maybe they've noticed my Gainesville hat and figure I must be the filmmaker. I walk past shocked faces reacting to seeing my mug in plain sight, quick double-takes, maybe it's my cane that's giving me away, maybe it's my overwhelming orange stink. I want to find out what the offer was. I see someone on the street, looks friendly, in the know, and stop to ask him if he knows which distributor bought The Gainesville Evidence?

"It wasn't Edgar," says the pod.

I'm not fast enough. Hurts to move around like this. I'm dead if I rest. I take a swig from the bodabag, passing the cigar store Indian on Main Street. Aliens have acquired Park City. Everyone in black recognizes me and stops to point at the recognizable limping wretch with a cane who betrayed their leader. Entrance to a restaurant called the Barking Frog beckons. What a name for the place where I died. Inside, I pay a temporary membership fee so I can drink and stare out the restaurant window at the shivering sidewalk crowd when my cell phone vibrates, ID: the fugitive's only friend.

"Franklin, can you hear me?"

"Yes I can Josh! Anything happen with your film? Is the abominable Edgar chasing after it?"

"We definitely are in play, Franklin. We're gonna close," I say.

"Did you get my (cough! cough!) rewrite to DQ?"

"He fell asleep, Franklin. You didn't help your case by giving me that Nabokov script! I gave it to his girlfriend and DQ somehow got hold of it, and it put him to sleep!"

"You're not making sense. Let's talk some other time, Josh. Perhaps when you are sober and coherent."

"Franklin, I'm not drunk. I'm on medication."

"Josh, you sound awful. Slurring something about Nabokov when the script I gave you was my rewrite! Where the hell is Lester? I can't believe (cough! cough!) he let you wander around so sick!"

"What rewrite?"

"The shooting script. Do you like the new title?"

"You gave me Infamous?"

"I thought you knew (cough! cough!). Josh, did you read it yet?"

I click off my cell. Well, that's the end of DQ for my movie. That's the end of Franklin in my life. Soon as I get back I'm going to shed him. No more expensing dinners, no more paying for everything. I push open the door to exit the Barking Frog—

"You fucking said last night to put it in writing!"

I want to say something to Edgar, but nothing comes out.

"You're going to need an army of lawyers after I'm through with you."

"You must have me mistaken for someone in a position

to even be at the same condo party as you."

Edgar laughs, appreciating the baldness of my lie.

"Are you a fucking kidder? Is that who you fucking think you are?"

I can feel Edgar's breath he's so in my face about Gainesville. I am not hallucinating any of this. Edgar is shouting into my eyeballs.

"Do you have any idea what I'm going to do to you?"

I am shaking like Janet Reno. The Barking Frog hostess suggests we take this discussion outside.

"Discussion? This is not a discussion, this is history."

Edgar stomps over to a dessert cart and returns to throw me up against the entryway of the Barking Frog.

"Kid, I'm going to make you fucking famous."

Edgar pastes my face with a Key Lime pie, smushing whipped cream and fresh cherries into my nostrils and mouth. I wipe graham cracker crust out of my eyes. Edgar struts across the restaurant to join his table. I stand accursed.

Sucking vodka out of the cuffs of my long sleeved shirt, the cold outside hardens the sticky sugar like pancake makeup. I'm wearing enough lime on my face I could make a pretty strong Gimlet. My cane slips and, angrily, I swing it against a parking meter, bending the aluminum, hampering my return to the condo, beyond bruised, just beyond. I am beyond. Back at the base, I open the door to the condo when I am hit with the room's cooked air and gusts of conversation of 50 people. Paul Oakenfold is deejaying some techno nonsense. Someone hands me a plastic cup of vodka, rocks; I take a sip, spit and spray it out, march towards the war room where the door is ominously closed. People I don't give a fuck about get in my way. I wish they would all just leave so I can go to sleep. They're going to be here all night and what is it, only five o'clock? I have to know how little we got for Gainesville. I'm trying to get to Lester Barnes and his attentive circle of Warners executives, cutting through the mass of models and actresses and dancing acquisition assistants, screaming "I Will Survive!" The circle opens, only slightly receptive to me. I realize I've probably crossed, cancelled on, and been dishonest with every executive in this circle except the Mormon executive named Brigham—

"You passed on Infamous," I remind the Mormon.

"I passed on the cop draft way back when. Franklin Brauner's a genius."

"Cop draft?"

"Brigham's bringing Franklin into the studio next week to discuss a couple projects before he gets completely unavailable," says Lester.

"You guys better be nice to him when he's over there. Don't send my client on a goose chase in the hot sun looking for the executive building."

"Been a while since Franklin's eaten at a commissary," says Lester,

"Who the hell would eat at the commissary?"

"What's a commissary?"

The Warners crew explodes with laughter. I throw away my cane like I'm at a revivalist meeting. Jessica is all chummy with Nazarian on the couch. I detour towards them and ask the agent to give me an update.

"Man, I'm off-duty. Go get your money from your buddy Lester," he says.

"Bramley, just tell me: how fucked was the offer?"

"Jesus Christ you smell like a chewy fruit roll."

"Congratulations, Josh, I heard you got a really good deal," says Jessica.

"Yeah? Well nobody told—"

I lunge at Nazarian. Who hits me in the face when he sees me about to strike. The women shriek at the sudden violence. I swing at him, miss my shot. The guys in the room quickly pull us away from each other. The whole thing is over in like ten seconds. Some jerk tells me to leave. I say, it's my fucking party, you leave! I limp to the fridge to get some ice for my swollen cheek, flecks of key lime pie around my neck, tangerine cologne smelling up the kitchen. Vietnamese manicurist grabs me by the elbow and I almost deck her.

"Hey there! Do you want to go somewhere now like my room to talk about that script Lester gave me?"

"Start over!"

"Did Edgar ever find you?"

"Tell me who ended up getting it, who's distributing!"

"Cinema Shares got it," she says.

"But they're a video company."

"They have a huge library. Now they're called Artesian. Do you have any grin on you? Why'd you hit Bramley? I mean, God, he only made you a million dollars!"

"We got a million dollars for Gainesville?"

"Where've you been, at screenings? That totally sucks you missed it! Bramley was awesome on the Searchlight business affairs call while Brad was closing with Cinema Shares."

"Fucking Nazarian!"

"Well, you made out. You're Lester's partner," she says.

"Yeah, right. I am so fucked."

"You're not fucked, you're family! Let's go find Lester!"

The 'war room' portal opens, revealing three men and a script on the bed. Shockingly sandwiched between Lester and Benny Pantera, DQ looks up from the pages of Dark Matter—

"Well, well, if it isn't Richard III," says DQ.

"I got pied at The Barking Frog!"

"He pied you? Edgar pied you!"

"What's he doing here?" I go, ticked off at Benny's presence.

"Is that Key Lime in your ears? I love Key Lime, let me taste that," says DQ.

"Don't do that!"

"Jeez. Kid's selfish."

DQ holds up the script. Like it's gold.

"Is Dick Donner's movie still in a holding pattern?"

"Lester. Can I have a minute?"

I'm in the bathroom next to the war room. Lester washes his hands.

"Feeling guilty about something?"

"What's on our mind, Josh?"

"Funny you should say 'our' mind, Lester. You know, like 'our' film. The one you sold without me, the one I brought you!"

"I don't have the jaws of life on me right now Josh, so spit out whatever is stuck in your pie-hole!"

"Did you just fuck me?"

"I would say, minus the commission, minus the lawyer bill, minus the cost of hiring Paul Oakenfold to do 'our' Gainesville party, you're about a million dollars fucked. Have Brad send the deal I papered and read the fine fucking print. Now if you'll excuse me, I have to go back in there to deal with 'our' foreign sales partner who's going to fully finance Infamous because DQ loves 'our' script."

"Franklin rewrote it. He changed the title to Dark Matter."

"That guy. Worse than a piece of tape, it's his draft DQ likes! You promised Franklin he could direct, didn't you!"

"What's a promise but words in the air?"

I feel cold, dead inside.

"What did you tell Edgar?"

"Lester, the screening we had was a disaster," I say.

"That ceiling? Some Lionsgate person got hurt!"

"I made sure there were no bootlegs."

"Edgar heard about our high school premiere. One of the kids camcorded it off the screen," says Lester.

"Tape quality must have been unwatchable."

"All Edgar saw was the crowd losing their popcorn!"

Lester leaves to go find some grin. All I think about is what the cigar store Indian said.

Greeting me at the door of her Studio City shanty, Dupin looks like a survivor of some terrible holocaust. A not-so-hot complexion. Chapped reindeer nose. Even her teeth are dirtier since the last time I saw her, which I honestly cannot remember when—

"Took me a while to find this place. Lots of lefts and rights," I say.

"This is what the top looks like! Come check out the motherfucking view!"

"Strawberry or banana tonight?"

Reason I ask is because Dupin's stringy black hair is damp around her face. Her brow is dotted with tiny sweat beads, like a boxer's face in the 8th round.

"Ossifer, take me away!"

Dupin snorts, melodramatically offers me both her wrists as if I'd brought over cuffs and a Miranda warning. She laughs, a high-pitched burp. I detest the sound, but I ignore it, feign a smile, and step onto her balcony: the lamps and billboards of Ventura Boulevard below.

"I can't believe you haven't been here yet," she says.

"Amazing view. For the Valley ."

"Oh fuck you, everyone loves the 'MGM' crib."

I move through the living room, where I step on remote controls for TiVo, Playstation 2, X-Box 360 on an impressive Polar Bear skin rug, test the overstuffed chairs in front of a widescreen TV.

"Is that an entertainment center or what? I can write it off now I'm a writer."

Dupin snuffs her nose with her sleeve, soaked with snot.

"Do you need an accountant, Josh? You should use mine, he's the goddamn greatest, and his little daughter Ella's just the sweetest thing!"

"Let's open this bottle of wine first. I want a tour of the crib."

"My crib! Yes, it's my crib! Come see the kitchen!"

The kitchen: totally modern and white. Butcher's block framed by hanging brass colanders, pots and pans. I notice two Cuisinarts, a juicer, trash compactor, and some futuristic thing I decide must be the toaster.

"Did you get married and divorced?"

"I fucked a guy last week, so shut up," she says.

Like it was a terrible meal. Dupin lights up a thin black cigarette whose brand escapes me at the moment, and I instantly send my brain on a name-search and rescue mission, coming up with: More. I'm pleased with myself.

"I can't wait to read Franklin's polish."

No way was I going to tell Dupin that it wasn't her script anymore. Franklin had taken a rib from her premise of a futuristic madman on the trail of a female detective, and made the skip tracer from the future a woman. He rewrote "Anton Sander" as this funny, misunderstood killer who falls head over heels in love with the victim he has targeted to die. The two women join forces to outfuck Sander in a supermarket showdown, letting the madman return to the future with the hope that he has been so changed by the experience, maybe he won't get the idea to time-travel, and if he does, it would be for an entirely different purpose. It was an 'Everybody Wins' ending that I found shocking, smart, and totally subversive.

"What happened to your B.C.P.D. pitch at 20th?"

Holding a full wine glass, Dupin hops up backwards on a tiled kitchen counter, doesn't spill a drop.

"Bramley said (sniff! sniff!) they shot a 'Caveman

Cops' pilot that didn't get picked up."

"I thought that Ron Bass thing at DreamWorks was yours."

"Somebody else got it. Roommate's boyfriend, I don't know. I faxed over the beat sheet last week."

"Oh no, sweetheart, they're going to use it, you should know better than to fax your brain to the nitwits!"

"I'm a slut. I'm such a slut—"

"Why'd you give it up so easily?"

"I just wanted Brit and Sonja to like me."

"Brit and Sonja don't like anyone, at the end of the day, behind their backs, they bad-mouth each other! They work this sexual shtick into every meeting."

"I desperately need a new laptop, Josh: Nosebleeds."

"Image: Beyond words. Save up for a new nose—"

Dupin's face explodes with sobs and snot. I want to comfort her, but my glass needs filling.

"Oh Josh, it's so not funny. I think I'm full of shit. I'm hopelessly untalented. There are hundreds of writers out there who are better than I am. More in demand than I am. Cuter and more fun than I am."

"Stop it, for Christ's sake, will you stop?"

"I'm not high-maintenance, I'm really not. Am I? I smoke all night. I stare at my laptop in bed. I get high. I go out on meetings. I spend more time at the studios than I do at home. I do all this work for people I don't even like, on other people's scripts, and when I don't get the assignment, I'm told: 'Sorry, we really liked your take, but we went with Mita & McClain because they have a movie coming out.' You know I found my dad after he ate a bullet for a midnight snack."

"Stop that talk. Right now. Or I'm leaving."

"No! Please don't do that, guru! No tough love, I can't handle it."

Dupin snuffs her nose.

"Is this why you came over? To tell me I have to write a spec? I knew it!"

"Tell me about your family. Your Dad was a cop."

"So was my Mom. So was my Grandfather."

"I love it, cop family! Why don't you write that?"

"You want Ordinary People, with my father's suicide? A little Good Will Hunting, or something you can set up at Lifetime?"

"How did your older brother turn out?"

"Divorced. Bitch wife got the kids. He was a cop, too. Narcotics, Monrovia."

"What if it was a family of cops? Let's say this crimelord really had it in for them, after the father sent him away to prison," I say.

"What if it's not just a psychopath who terrorizes a family of cops, what if it was a 'family' of convicts who break out, like the Texas 7, open with a jailbreak set-piece, they all want Dad dead," she says.

"Does this family of cops have a dog?"

"A K-9, like Beethoven!"

"So: Mom wants to leave Dad, asking herself: Is that all there is?"

"Dad's retired, desperate for excitement in his life again," says Dupin.

"And the baby of the family, the sister, just graduated from Academy. Nobody in the family takes her seriously. They still call her Peanut."

"I got it! We get Clint Eastwood to play the Grandfather."

"That's genius, I smell refund," I say.

"Maybe he's got terminal cancer and Pops hasn't told anyone in the family he's dying so he's reckless!"

"Lethal Weapon with a Walker."

"Climax takes place on Thanksgiving Day. Family shines, comes together, kills the convicts, but Pops takes one in the chest."

On the kitchen TV: A promo for KCAL-9 news: BREAKING NEWS – SUSPECT EXONERATED – CONFESSION COERCED.

"The next time this family has Thanksgiving, they don't call her Peanut. They call her lieutenant—"

"No fucking way!"

"You don't think it'll sell, Josh?"

"Look! That guy who confessed was bullshit!"

On the TV, attorney Gloria Allred is holding a press conference flanked by the WILL SCREENWRITE FOR FOOD guy and Rodney King.

"Bramley says Curtis Hansen is looking to do a family film at Universal—"

"Why would this guy confess and then say he didn't do it?"

"Guru! There's a big bag of money on the table! Do you think this will sell?"

"Is he going to be on Larry King? Does this guy think he'll get an assignment out of the notoriety? Who's on Jerry's case now?"

"Can we stop talking about your fucking brother?"

"I don't have a brother anymore—"

I throw down my napkin. Eye the front door.

"Detective."

Driving down Billy Wilder Boulevard, I notice a white Humvee limousine in my rear-view mirror. My cell phone vibrates: It's Franklin, who demands to know why Lester has been in Hawaii for weeks. I was initially pissed when Lester and Franklin excluded me from their first meeting with DQ at Anarkali. Lester said my presence there would be like "tits on a nun," but I got over the brush-off real quick when it was announced Franklin had somehow convinced the movie star to let him direct. Franklin launches a bilious diatribe about the disgusting notes on his script by the "miscreants" who toil for Benny Pantera, the marginal casting directors they're making him use, actors he would never even consider, could give a fuck about their "foreign" value.

"I'm told they need a new title to sell foreign. Dark Matter doesn't play."

"So go back to the original title," I say.

"Infamous doesn't sell it either. They need the word 'Time' in the title for the buyers to understand they're getting a (cough! cough!) time-travel movie."

"Little on the nose, don't you think, Franklin?"

"I need a title, guru. Or our movie is going to be served in Scandinavia dripping with cheese."

"How about Killing Time?"

"Can't say 'Kill.' Tried that."

"Wait, Franklin, some asshole's cutting into my lane without signaling—I got it! Let's take a line from the script and give it to the title."

White Humvee limousine ominously rides my tail.

"Something about the script's sexuality, something that combines the wild love story of these two women and Sander's brutality," I say.

"Wild's good."

"I got it! I got it, Franklin: Wild Time."

"Wild Time, yes—"

"Hold it! Lester on the other line! Call you back," I say.

I click off Franklin, click on for Lester: "Catch your first tube yet?"

It's Lester's assistant, placing the call for him.

"Hey Lester, someone's following me in a limo."

"It's Bob Kosberg, he wants to pitch you. Are we alone?"

His voice sounds weird. Fragile.

"You sound sick."

The Humvee limo shadows me down Maple Drive, turns right on Wilshire Boulevard, maintains a steady pursuit.

"Get off my ass! Lester, I need you to write down a license plate. I think this limo's been following me."

"Josh, I don't have a pen."

"Well, ask one of the waitresses by the pool where you're at!"

"You're not being followed, stop being so dramatic."

"I'm on Olympic now, Lester! I can't shake him!"

"Life is not always a movie, Josh!"

"Help me get down the plate number! A as in Alpha, the number 4—"

Traffic light at Olympic and Sawtelle looms green, which means: Go.

"I don't have a pen. I'm not in Hawaii right now."

Cars speed up, because the light turns yellow: Go Faster.

"You're location scouting," I say.

I punch the gas pedal, squeeze the lemon.

"I'm at UCLA."

Behind me, cars jerk to a halt, horns detonate, fenders collide. In my mirror, the gorgon is left to idle at the light.

"What, tonight's class speaker bailed? Lester, I've been waiting for you to ask—"

"I'm at UCLA Medical Center."

I feel the vastness of mortality standing on my chest when I enter the library-quality stillness of UCLA Medical Center, touch a computer screen to hunt for Lester's location in the hospital, type in the word "Barnes," and clip on an orange visitor's pass for ICU. I ride up an elevator filled with waste carts and stunned, mute family members until I step out to Lester's floor. I push open the hospital room without knocking, dark in here. I've just walked in on something. Did I see that? What was that nurse just doing? I can't see Lester's face. Standing over the bed holding a pillow, this fucked-up nurse couldn't look any guiltier. Was she thinking what I'm thinking she was about to do? Am I imagining things, or was this tall nurse for just a split-second fantasizing about smothering Lester with his own pillow? Would she receive a commission? I should have brought flowers, but he didn't need them. Lester is flatlining. The monitors go berserk. Alarms detonate, nurses and a black doctor bump past me, slide a board under Lester Barnes, who isn't breathing. The scene reminds me of Alien Autopsy. One of the nurses pulls his head back by the hair, opens his jaw so she can slide a tube down his throat: "Give him another Epi!" No one notices me in the doorway; they're busy booking Lazarus: "You put the foley in him!" A hand feeds a catheter into Lester's chubby penis as he goes involuntary with his bowels: “Somebody get out the lido!” Another charging nurse directs me out of the room when the black doctor proclaims to the heavens: “Alive! He’s Alive!”

You think you're in heaven but really you're just going to the ultimate premiere and after-party. You have Lester's tickets and Jerry's tux and your limo driver Boston looks exactly like Magic Johnson when he smiles. You bring your own Mandrin instead of the Stoli provided in the stretch. You feel bad you snubbed Dupin, not taking her tonight, lying about where you're going, hoping she's working on her spec instead of watching TV. You're in heaven because your date, Carmen, smells like a confectionary. You decline to eat her dress, wishing it wasn't made entirely out of black licorice whips. You hate licorice more than anything. Your date, sucking on a Black Vine, looking at you from across the way, hair and makeup done by a professional who worked on Home Improvement, knocks her knees together with excitement as you turn onto Hollywood Boulevard. Your limousine is swarmed by signs everywhere protesting the Best Costume Design nomination for "The Turner Diaries." You stare at graphic, poignant posters of relatives and children lost in the Oklahoma City Bombing. You skipped the "Turner" premiere so you don't know why these people are decrying Hollywood's irresponsibility. National Guardsmen everywhere point assault rifles, protecting you from another encroaching row of mostly white haired octogenarians who oppose the honorary Oscar being given tonight to "Natan the Namer," the screenwriter Natan Volonsky, who informed on all his friends back in the day. One of the old guys gets clipped by Boston's side view mirror as your limo pulls up to the first wave of security checkpoints at Hollywood & Highland and the Academy Awards. Carmen tells you to slow down because it's the Oscars and you're rushing to get inside the place. You feel the sun on your forehead, but your eyes are blinded by the red carpet. You've never seen anything so hellishly red as the velvet under your feet.

You move through the metal detectors. All you hear is a loud buzz of traffic, lots of shouting, and cheers from the stands across the street from the Kodak Theatre. Carmen's twizzler chainmail barely covers her breasts. Her eyelids are encrusted with chocolate nonpareils that make you think of Alicia Keys. You come over to Carmen, whose candy outfit has caught the attention of the media. Clickclickclick. "What designer are you wearing?" Clickclickclick. You see yourself reflected in the lens of an ACCESS HOLLYWOOD camera. Clickclickclick. You hear Carmen talk about edible couture and introduce you to the world as her "Guru." You want to reach for your flask, but you put it away when you realize you're going to be on camera as long as you walk on the red carpet. You climb the red staircase, passing a pair of gigantic Oscar statues, notice lighted columns with names of movies you know but have never seen, until the 1990's column of movies start to appear and you realize these are the names of Oscar's Best Pictures.

You know absolutely nobody at this party. Nobody comes up to you. You're looking for a life preserver in the middle of a wide-open ocean. You've lost Carmen. Your flask is your only friend. You think you see people you know and the one familiar face in the crowd is the cigar store Indian from Park City. You cut though a thick wall of backless dresses as the cigar store Indian from Park City points out Carmen, surrounded by a CAA mob. You hear Carmen thank them for their interest, move towards the "guy in her life." That's you. We take our seats. Nobody waves in our direction. We're the only ones in our row sitting; everyone else is schmoozing in the aisles. You're filled with awe and wonder and respect and that's when you start to lose feeling in your hands. You count the number of balconies high above the rows of seats until you look up so high your neck is almost turned all the way around. Your throat closes. Your head feels swollen and tingly. Carmen, sensing your panic attack, takes your hand and holds it. Then, Bill Conti nukes the orchestra.

Winona wins Best Supporting Actress. Warren Beatty introduces the first Best Picture clip of the night, "Nude Nudes." Carmen nudges you during the clip about a doomed love story between a disfigured stripper and a lonely paralegal overcoming the odds until he dumps her after she sees him through law school. After an acoustic guitar rendition by Slash, nominated for best song from the film, "Conversations with a Cannibal," a majestic silver screen drops from the ceiling, lights dim until the Kodak is in total darkness and "In Memoriam" burns on screen. Clip of a drug addict's finest moment on film. Applause. More clips of dead people who lost their lives fighting the system, their addictions and their families before finally, stupidly, beating themselves. When they run a montage of stills of Hollywood victims without identification, you recognize Franklin Brauner on the screen. Maybe it was a clerical error. You're outraged. Bud Wiggins takes the statue for Best Original Screenplay. The 3rd Best Picture clip is introduced by Gore Vidal: "Handcarved Coffins." Peter Coyote announces a commercial break before the Oscar goes to Natan Volonsky. Seat fillers take your places as you and Carmen walk up the aisle to the lobby area, which is packed with more people than you expect, then you realize the reason it is getting so crowded is because nobody wants to be seen inside the auditorium when Natan the Namer accepts his award.

Your cell vibrates, ID: FRANKLIN.

"Franklin! Did you see it? You were at the Oscars—"

The auteur stops you cold.

"I'll be right there."

Franklin had been pulled over on Los Feliz Boulevard for a DWI: Driving While Insane. It wasn't the busted tail light that attracted the cop's attention, it was the bare-naked psycho at the wheel, singing along to Ruggero Leoncavallo's Pagliacci while zig-zagging across Echo Park Boulevard in a black Saab convertible.

"Said he wanted to talk to his guru. I thought maybe he was talking about the Bhagwan. Movie director, huh? One of our officers knows him from way back when, says he's one of those tormented geniuses who doesn't get the opportunities he used to anymore. You his lawyer?"

"No, I just, look, I barely know the guy. We're working on a few projects together."

"He had one phone call. He called you," says the desk captain.

"I'm just glad he didn't kill anybody," I say.

"Must be pretty important to make you leave the Oscars."

Emerging from a steel door, Franklin Brauner touches his dark blue jail uniform, wondering how the hell he ended up here in the first place. Carmen drapes my tuxedo jacket over his shoulders.

"I go to a lot of movies, my wife's a great picture picker at Blockbuster, but I wouldn't trust that guy to direct my son's 4th grade play."

Franklin's hair has seemingly turned white since the last time I saw him. Growing a goatee, his face is flecked with sharp white whiskers, making his face incredibly feline.

"Like the look, Franklin: Very Dr. Moreau."

"I'm making Sander an opera lover. Where do we stand on Maggie Gyllenhall?"

"Her agent passed. Everybody passed, Franklin. No one wants to do it."

"Have you seen Dick Donner hanging around the lobby lately?"

"Stop it, Franklin. You're the director until somebody says you're not."

"Who's the pencil on my deal?"

"Brad Blumberg," I say.

"Perfect. He represents everybody. Jew eat?"

Skipping the governor's ball, I tell Boston to drive us over to Thai Elvis. Over naked shrimp and deep fried trout, Carmen and the director talk about sex, music videos they admire, and her dead father. Franklin says he wants to put Carmen on tape at his house. In the parking lot, Boston suggests he'll wait for us after we're done. I ask Boston if he knows something we don't, and he says he took Whitney Houston "up there" once before, to Franklin's lair.

I walk into Lester getting a handjob from this really cute TA from his class at UCLA, who introduces herself as his niece before she leaves the room. Lester smiles wolfishly, but it doesn't change the decades catching up to his looks with a vengeance. His hair is clumpy in places. IV's and tubes connected to machines that monitor every flickering electrical drumbeat from his chest. Lester feels a chill, adjusts his equipment under the covers.

"Did you know DQ jumped out of a plane last week because Franklin said Sander is an adrenaline addict? They've spent so much time together I wouldn't put it past them if they're fuck buddies," says Lester.

"What's with the cross country trip?"

"Whatever's good for the project. Like I'm going to tell him he can't drive through America so he can find his character? He's brainwashed my client. I've done fifteen movies with DQ. This picture, I'm telling you, frightens me."

Littered with glossy magazines over his hospital bed, Entertainment Weekly nominates Carmen Coronado on the cover for an edible Oscar.

"I brought you a DVD," I say.

"Porn? I can't handle porn right now."

"This is the most passed around audition tape in Hollywood."

"Player's over there. I had the nurses put in my own entertainment center after my staph infection."

On the big-screen TV set up in the hospital room, Franklin's viewfinder reveals Carmen and I sitting across from each other on stools, holding script pages, rehearsing in our Oscar outfits. My bowtie is undone, tuxedo shirt open. Carmen is sucking a rope of licorice, only she's basic naked instead of basic black. We run through the scene where Carmen's character explains what it's like to discover the jolt of attraction towards a woman as the camera zooms in to capture the arousal purpling Carmen's cheeks—

SCREEN INTERNATIONAL

GENERALISSIMO TAKES "TIME OUT"

SANTA MONICA – Hong Kong and Amsterdam-based Generalissimo Film Sales has extended its relationship with producer Benny Pantera, snapping up sales rights to the $44 million DQ thriller "Time Out."

"Independents are dependent on adventurous audiences," said Lester Barnes from Cedars-Sinai's ICU.

Project, which stars DQ as a time-traveling serial killer and fiery newcomer Carmen Coronado as the object of his obsession, will be produced by Barnes, Pantera (The Mighty Mite, Ajax), and Guru's Josh Makos.

"Every now and then, I've got to satisfy parts of myself that only satisfy myself," stresses DQ, who joins the growing list of major stars in films put together by Omniscience's Independent Film Division who have enjoyed the kind of creative control they have not had in studio movies.

"Time Out" starts shooting March 15 in Wilmington, Delaware. Franklin Brauner directs. Calls to Makos were not returned.

I have one rule when I'm on set: Say Nothing. I wear a headset, hang out by the video monitor, tell the P.A. to bring me a water bottle so I can go to my trailer and fill it with Mandrin. I stay away from the craft service table. "That's how Marlon got fat," according to Franklin, who's not doing too well in this first week of production. He refuses to shave, or bathe, and he's turned mean. DQ is driving across the United States, late to work. Only Lester Barnes and Franklin are kept apprised of which state he's passing through. Benny Pantera's handpicked line producer makes a mortal enemy out of the director by breaking for lunch just when the camera blocking is going smoothly and the actors are starting to really cook. When the line producer threatens to cut his shooting days, everybody on set witnesses Franklin tear a handful of pages out of the script:

"Now we're three days ahead of schedule! Happy?"

The phone rings inside the du Pont screening room where Franklin is running dailies. Benny Pantera answers it, snaps his fingers to stop the screening, and the room realizes the caller is DQ from the road.

"He only wants to talk to you, Franklin," says Benny.

Franklin listens to the movie star and whispers into the phone so we can't hear him. Franklin hangs up and winds his way back to his seat.

"What did he want?" asks the line producer.

"He wanted to know if he could wear a dress," replies Franklin.

"I hope you told him no," says the line producer.

"You tell him no, that's what you're good at," says the director.

"Why the drive? He can afford his own plane, what bullshit!"

"He's finding his character," explains Franklin.

"Deep," Line producer snorts at the screen. "Too bad Carmen can't act."

"Why are you even here?" screams Franklin.

The projectionist is signaled, our screen flickers with the last of the day's shots. We watch a digital slate thrust into frame, over Franklin's incessant coughing off camera.

"Let's replace her before DQ shows up," says the line producer.

"You can get yourself another director if you do that!"

"She stinks, Franklin," declares Benny Pantera.

"Go clean money or whatever it is you do while the rest of us are on set."

In the dark, the room admires the first scene we shot between Carmen and Ling-Ling, a world-renowned actress of Chinese stage and screen, who had agreed to play the skip tracer "Victoria," Carmen's passion, and Sander's omni-sexual nemesis. There were clashes between Franklin, the producers, and Generalissimo Films over this particular piece of casting. Ling-Ling wanted to work with Franklin, but she had recently discovered she was pregnant, which meant she only had a few weeks to shoot her part, which meant futzing with the shooting schedule. Franklin fought for Ling-Ling's participation and won, but her casting cost him some days. Franklin's allergies are so terrible the sound guy complains he can't hear the actors with Franklin constantly coughing, so the sadistic line producer banishes Franklin to direct from behind a video monitor inside the toilet of the Brandywine Valley stages. Isolated from the crew, the despised director blocks with the D.P. and forgets to eat his lunch.

I say very little to Franklin when I'm on set. I don't want to hang out by those urinals. Line producer wants to break for supper. The D.P. is out of smokes, about to lose it. Carmen keeps missing her mark, failing to stop on a piece of silver duct tape on the floor, motivating the camera to follow her and push right up to her face, which is supposed to look terrified. Carmen's bisexual heroine has just been date-raped twice, and she's having difficulty summoning the tears on cue. Draped over a director's chair, Ling-Ling plays with her yo-yo. The D.P. throws a hissy fit when the line producer tells him he's only got one more, maybe two takes, to get this right. Members of the crew idle by the craft service table, but not the restroom: that's where Franklin and Carmen huddle with each other. Franklin isn't about to resort to vegetables, but I'm beginning to doubt my director when I hear—Slap! Slap! The bathroom door opens, revealing a rosy-cheeked Carmen. Franklin calls out "Action!" Carmen hits her mark, acts "upset," but she's still not believable enough for anyone to think she's even dismayed. Carmen folds her arms, defiant. Franklin emerges from the toilet, fuming with authoritative rage. Ling-Ling is about to make a suggestion when Franklin slaps Carmen's face and asks for a fresh slate. Within seconds, we're ready. This time Carmen hits her mark and nails it. Ling-Ling drops her yo-yo and scrambles to retrieve it when—Slap! Slap! Carmen bursts into tears—Slap! Slap!

"Stop this! Right now! Somebody get the producer," exclaims Ling-Ling.

The entire crew turns to watch Franklin take on the Chinese bitch.

"What the fuck is wrong with you, Franklin? I've worked with some unprofessional directors, some real tyrants, but we actors have to do something when we see abuse!"

"Ling-Ling, she's not a pro," says Franklin.

"That doesn't call for you to hit her!"

"You don't understand, Carmen wants me to hit her."

Ling-Ling turns to her co-star. Carmen says True, with her eyes.

"It's the only way we can get the shot off," says Franklin.

"She wants you to hit her."

"Yes, Ling-Ling."

There's this long beat of reflection from Ling-Ling.

"Can I have a crying scene?"

Franklin's laugh catches in his throat when a P.A. hands him a cell phone.

"It's Anton Sander."

Unexpectedly arriving on the set, DQ's frightening presence induces nervousness and silence. The movie star has gone gaunt, his face shockingly bone white, strange sigils tattooed around the back of his shaved head complete with a futuristic goatee, bunched up, tied into pointy knots. His performance on the first day, waging a destructive war against anybody who was not the director, nearly causes production to face a shutdown. Every serf on the crew looks away when the dark lord is on set. Shooting his entrance scene, "Anton Sander" arrives, a long way from a far future, naked, on the run, and erect. Thinking nothing of it, DQ throws down his bathrobe and panthers around bare-assed in front of Franklin and the crew. After the first take, Franklin encourages the actors to stretch out their lines, giving them "free" takes to try things, imbue their performances with unexpected spontaneity that only emerges from being in the moment. DQ punches in a few numbers on what looks like a cell phone but is actually the worm hole navigator prototype that Sander, a Cal Tech janitor, stole from a lab 200 years from now. Carmen, playing "Daisy James," behind the wheel of a cherry Mustang convertible, pulls up alongside a sprinting Sander, who's just saved her from "Victoria," in hot pursuit of her fugitive, but which one is the futuristic skip tracer really after?

No longer speaking to one another, Franklin and the producers childishly use the 1st A.D. as their pigeon to convey hostile messages back and forth. With the late arrival of DQ to the shoot, I can no longer Say Nothing. I now have a new rule: Scream Louder. Jessica was pissed off at me that I didn't fight to get her a lowly P.A. position so I flew her to Wilmington and made her "assistant to Carmen Coronado." When I wanted to put her up at the Hotel du Pont, where DQ was staying under the name Archie Leach, the line producer screamed he would only pay for the Holiday Inn on Concord Pike, with the rest of the "crew." So I got in his face and Screamed Louder that I would take care of Jessica on "my own card!" Scream Louder, and people on the set will think you are a crazy person feeling pressure they can't begin to imagine. Shit that's your problem becomes someone else's now that nobody wants to deal with you.

Storming off the set over wardrobe, DQ fires the unit publicist caught staring at him, the "Edith Hag" costumer from Paris, and "that bitch script supervisor" before stopping to urinate on the side of his trailer in front of the camera crew shooting the E.P.K, 'Time Out with DQ,' for the planned Criterion Collection DVD. As the end of the movie star's first week neared, I, the star wrangler, facetiously suggested at an emergency production meeting perhaps it would be cheaper to start a titty bar in DQ's trailer. The joke was lost on the line producer, who subsequently bought an entire block of streetwalkers for the star's pleasure just so the crew could get back to telling stories with pictures. Walking through the honey wagons and trucks at base camp, I never see the prostitutes during the shoot, only glimpses of their hair, blinking eyes and orange cigarette embers through the door of DQ's star wagon. DQ's no-shows on the set forced Franklin and the producers to use 'Sander' stunt doubles. The line producer would gladly kick in DQ's teeth, but he needs him to start showing up. DQ thinks everybody's nothing except for Franklin. On set, Franklin fantasizes about pulling off the line producer's eyelids and pouring in scalding hot coffee, but first, finish the film. Benny Pantera and Franklin? All slaps on the back, and you never saw a phonier act of friendship anywhere. Every character is on edge, all the time, then there's a blowup on set, and the producers, dollar signs for pupils, link arms against the director and the star, flexing their droit moral muscles, bayonets at the ready.

Never order a beer in Delaware, ask for a Midas. Praised by archeologists and drunks alike, the local micro-brewery produces almost 10,000 barrels of "Midas Touch Golden Elixir" a year. Using ingredients from the king's 2,699-year old tomb, legend has it this fearsome ale turned King Midas's funeral into a bacchanalia that drew so many souls, even Hades with Persephone got turned away. At the local Kahunaville, the entire Time Out crew has taken over this island-themed restaurant. Inside its tropical garden, indoor waterfalls surround a stage where an aging cover band fronts a singer who reminds me of Juice Newton. Channeling Peter O'Toole from Night of the Generals, Franklin enters Kahunaville with Carmen and Jessica on his arms, pushing their heads together, encouraging the vixens to make public their display of affection. I'm on my fourth Mandrin and the girl singer on stage is doing her Janis Joplin thing. DQ barges past the bouncers, sweaty, out of breath. The house band goads the movie star to join them on stage. DQ throws off his leather jacket, revealing a tight, black T-shirt advertising the lunch special from No Discretion. Possessed by "Sander," the idol takes the stage in full-blown character. DQ snatches a guitar out of the house musician's hands, orders him to fuck off, intimidates the star-struck band to follow his lead, and rips into the opening chords of "Jane Says." The Wilmingtons leap from their barstools to the dance floor, worshipping DQ on his altar, pawing his boots and Kahunaville becomes a buzzing hive.

On set, Franklin is directing from the toilet, laughing

whenever "Sander" has a scene with "Daisy James." DQ is playing the part of infatuated dope to the hilt. Between setups, Carmen and Jessica, her giggling, inseparable companion, ask crew members if they're "boxers or briefs?" When DQ fails to show up in the afternoon, the line producer goes off on the 1st A.D. "Find him! We need him yesterday!" 1st A.D. shrieks in front of everybody on set that I go find DQ. I Scream Louder: Why the fuck should I know where "Sander" is? I have no fucking idea why he isn't on set. I'm not his mother. If it makes you fucking happy I'll look for him myself. Warty twat.

I peel out of another strip joint parking lot, hunting a movie star without a fucking clue. The line producer heard DQ got violent outside the club No Discretion on the first night he came to town, but he wasn't there today. I pull into a ratty strip club called Pom-Poms and the place is going off with lights, smoke, and Aerosmith. Sloppy table dancers gyrate over lonely shlubs, while a few girls in better shape take a break, watching the girl with no pubes on a pole, tipping their own strain. I make my way over to the brass rail, where DQ pitches Andrew Jackson fastballs at Miss Innocent on stage, who couldn't really be 18, could she? The movie star fans himself with a bushel of cash, flicks his head.

"Nice ham," says DQ.

Miss Innocent gives him the finger. Movie star laughs. I take a seat.

"I always liked you," the movie star laughs, "and your brother."

"What's with the past tense?" I ask DQ, sensing danger.

"Hey Mabel, bring us two shot glasses and a bottle of Jack," he says.

"Scratch that order. I'm not drinking any Jack and neither are you."

"Fuck you talking about?"

"Bring us a bottle of Mandrin."

DQ slaps my back, delighted with my spontaneity, tips her twenty.

"How's that Noelle treating you?"

"She slept with our yoga instructor. Want her number now?"

"You kidding? I know where she's been," I say.

The music stops. Movie star milks the moment, then he cracks up, revealing lots of little wrinkles all over his face.

"My brother Jerry said you guys hung out all the time."

"'Stop all the clocks, cut off the telephone, prevent the dog from barking with a juicy bone, silence the pianos and with muffled drum, bring out the coffin, let the mourners come.'"

"Tell me a story. Make it good," I say.

"Which one do you want to hear, how your brother was fucking Lester's wife, ending their marriage, or the time he house sat for Lester and Benny Pantera ended up shooting 'The World's Biggest Bukkake' on his tennis court?"

Mandrin arrives. I pour us doubles.

"Did Lester care about his wife?"

"It was more about the principle. Kid gave Lester the bump when he could've been somebody, but it wasn't his night," says DQ.

"At the Silent Movie Theatre?"

"No, that night in the Garden," he says.

"I'm sorry, you lost me."

"You remember that night in the Garden. You said, 'Kid, this ain't your night.' My night? I could've taken Wilson apart! I could have gotten a shot at the title, instead of a one-way ticket to Palookaville."

"Now you're fucking with me," I say.

"Step on my line when I say 'Palookavile.' Say, 'I put

some bets down, you saw some money.' Say it, ready? 'I could have gotten a shot at the title, instead of a one-way ticket to Palookaville—"

"I put some bets down, you saw some money—"

"You don't understand! You was my brother, Charlie! You should have taken care of me, you should've taken care of me just a little bit so I wouldn't have had to take them dives for the short-end money," he says.

"Who's Charlie? Finish your drink—"

"You don't understand! I could have been somebody. I could have had class! I could have been a contender, instead of a bum, which is what I am, let's face it."

Miss Innocent approaches the rail, bends over, spreads her cheeks, offers DQ a Sharpie through her legs—

"Would you mind autographing my asshole?"

Back on set, I head for the makeup trailer. I say good morning to the stylists when Carmen enters, steaming cup of coffee in hand, cigarette for breakfast, shaking her head.

"I just heard the most fucked up story."

Hair and makeup girls multi-task, all ears.

"Sound guy played me a recording. Remember that day they served clam chowder, DQ stole a car and stormed off?"

"The day he wouldn't say his lines," disses Makeup.

"Because he didn't think the scene was justified and felt the dialogue was redundant," adds Hair.

"Cup my balls. Stroke the shaft. Call me king," says Carmen.

The floor goes, "What?"

"Or was it, stroke my shaft, cup the balls and call me king?"

"This chick's lost her shit this morning," says Hair.

"Carmen, keep saying that, I'm gonna come," I say.

"That's what DQ kept saying over and over again to the hooker blowing him in his trailer. No idea he was still miked."

The stylists are laughing themselves silly when the 1st A.D. enters, walkie-talkie crackling: DQ just fired the director. Scene out of any war movie: Soldier screaming under heavy artillery fire, desperately relaying the details of a massacre to his superiors via walkie-talkie:

"He's leaving the hotel! DQ is driving away! Come back! Come back, DQ!"

People are crying their eyes out at the Holiday Inn on Concord Plaza. Crew members are furious, worried about getting paid, with the official word coming from the 1st A.D. that we are in shutdown until the replacement director arrives, that is, if we get one. The police came to the set earlier, to break up a fistfight between some local who hadn't been paid by the producers for the use of his house as a location and somebody in the accounting office. Wardrobe trucks drive off before they can be looted. Then, at an emergency production meeting held outside the soundstages, in front of the entire production, line producer announces DQ quit the movie and John Badham will not be stepping in. At the airport gate, Jessica kisses me goodbye and slips me her tongue while Carmen isn't looking before their flight back to L.A. Driving back to basecamp, I veer off Exit 95 to the screening room, where I know I'll find Franklin. Sitting in the front row, the exiled director is running dailies, admiring the film he got in the can, all thirteen shooting days worth of genius. I Say Nothing.

THE WILMINGTON INQUIRER

HOLLYWILD—Delaware is still in shock over the shutdown last weekend of the DQ-starrer "Time-Out." On Friday the movie star "axed" the director Franklin Brauner and his cinematographer to leave the tiny, no-sales-tax state. Crew members of the tanked and yanked-for-good shoot are crying over Midas beers, recounting true tales of terror about the actor's notorious disposition and generous support of the local prostitution community. Wilmington's Chancery Court, the Coliseum for corporate litigators, can expect to see DQ's name on their marquee versus local plaintiffs over unpaid locations, rentals, props, salaries, and a six-figure clean-up bill from the city's sanitation department. $tay tuned.

Lookout Mountain off Laurel. I'm driving to see Franklin, having just seen Lester to tell him the good news, but now I'm lost. How the fuck do you get up there again? I'm supposed to look for wizards, crescent moons; forks and knives painted on the parking curbs: secret directions to Franklin's house. It's raining for the first time since I came here for Jerry's funeral—

"No more working with auteurs, ever!" whispered Lester Barnes from his bedside at Cedars-Sinai, earlier today.

"I wouldn't put DQ in a room with any of them, not even Todd Haynes! It's time to get back to making meat and potato pictures!"

I told Lester I was tired from the experience.

"That movie was a bad call. I should have never trusted Franklin to direct anything, what was I thinking? He's done this to me before," said Lester.

"Who, DQ?"

"Franklin! Pay attention! I was his agent when he had Brando set in his picture! He could have directed Wicked Game with you know, what's her name, but he got fired when he pushed too hard for so-and-so from that bouncer movie!"

I told Lester he had it all wrong if he thought the collapse of the picture was Franklin's fault. Lester lifted up a corner of the oxygen mask to hiss:

"Why, you serpent's tooth!"

Lookout Mountain to Wonderland Ave, don't take Place. Follow the curb drawing Aleister Crowleys with little cone hat, starry cape, magic wand to Duffy Ave. I find Sunset Plaza Drive, careful not to drive off one of these cliffs.

"I worry about staph infections, not lawsuits! I've been to the other side, Josh. I was dead."

I asked the ex-agent, so then, what's after death?

"I don't know what's after your death. I only know what's after mine. Kay Coleman's pouring the coffee at Nate 'n Al's. All my friends are sitting in their booths, toasted bagels and smoked whitefish, lox and eggs, everybody reading Peter's column about DQ playing celebrity Jeopardy when the answer is 'Two Picture Deal' and Alex Trebek hears, 'Who I have to fuck to get off this movie?'"

"Two-picture deal?"

"I had a long talk with the studio. We're putting DQ on a flat-fee diet, totally Atkins."

According to Lester, the studio would acquire Generalissimo Films for their embryonic film library and expense the cremation of 'Time Out.' The movie star was now under contract for a pair of pictures, mutually agreed upon, in exchange for this multi-million dollar reprieve.

"They just messengered me this script they bought last week, heard of it? Hockey player addicted to pills, illiterate waitress raising a child prodigy alone, they fall in love, somebody dies, broke every reader's heart on the lot!"

"Holy shit, DQ got Stanley's Cup?"

"My nurse, Carl: he thinks 'Oscar' came with the script. Take a look at it for DQ. I've been too busy with myocardial infarctions. I sent DQ to Promises so they can unfuck Franklin's mind trip. If you ever set foot again in the state of Delaware, they'll arrest you."

Franklin's in a good mood when I arrive. Inside: no music. Only the sound of rain plinking the roof. Curves of glass crunch under my shoes. Somebody recently threw wine on the walls. Through the window in Franklin's kitchen, I'm devastated by his view of Los Angeles. Every time I see her I fall in love. Holding a plate of huevos rancheros, Franklin starts talking about Nabokov, telling me about a meeting he had at the Glen with his neighbor, this retired sea captain, who liked Pale Fire and wants to help find the money. He mentions Bill Pullman has committed to play John Shade, U.K. film distributor Seamus says they're in, and ICM is being really helpful. My host offers me coffee, retrieves a stack of well-toasted egg bread out of the oven, burns his fingertips. Franklin asks if I want jam (cough! cough!) with my egg bread, I say sure. The director lights up a Camel Wide he finds half-smoked on the windowsill over the sink. I follow Brauner's liver-spotted hand holding the cigarette rising up to peeling-chapped lips. Shadows crisscross his face, at one point forming a blindfold. I'm staring at a wispy rope of yellow cheese stuck on his chin when the phone rings. Franklin lets it go. The ringing turns incessant.

"Creditors," I joke.

"That's not Citibank, it's Ling-Ling."

Franklin tells me the Chinese star of stage and screen miscarried after the shoot. I take a deep breath before I tell Franklin the fantastic news about the studio agreeing to bury his film, the two-picture deal, how everybody took the fucking money. I watch Franklin absorb the information. He stubs out his smoke. Clears the plates from the table. Exits. I'm intrigued by a picture frame on the wall in his kitchen, a prized portrait of somebody named Kenneth Anger by Francis Bacon when a gunshot erupts from the next room.

"Franklin, stop bleeding! We have to stop the bleeding! Oh God it's everywhere! Keep your eyes open, Franklin! Franklin! I'm calling 911!"

"911 is a joke," he says.

"I can't believe you're still alive! Here! Keep the towel over your forehead. Stop feeling that hole in your head! Stop it, Franklin! Yes! Operator! I need an ambulance now, now, now! Hollywood Hills, my best friend shot himself!"

"I wrote everything in a letter you'll find on the bed."

"Yes, he's still alive! Somebody get here quick! 7348 Sunset Plaza, at the very top of Sunset Plaza Drive! Follow the wizards on the curb, make sure they follow the wizards up to the house! Franklin, stop bleeding—"

"The Bacon's yours. Put my Saab on Craig's List—"

"I don't want any painting! Shut up! I can't believe you're still talking! Hold that towel! Keep it inside! Don't close your eyes, Franklin! Keep talking, stay awake, stay with me!"

"The only performance that makes it, that really makes it, that makes it all the way, is this one."

"Look at me! Franklin? Franklin? Franklin?"

"Jerry didn't finish the book."

"Franklin! Keep your eyes open!"

"The book finished him."

"You have Jerry's book? Franklin!"

"It's in there: Everything. His death, his killer—"

"Keep talking, Franklin, keep your eyes open! Where is the goddamn ambulance! Quit that! You're still bleeding!

I'm calling 911 again!"

"A 'non-pro.' Not of the Industry. A salesman—"

"Operator! Yes, this is 7348 Sunset Plaza Drive! No, the paramedics haven't arrived. Yes, he's still talking, still bleeding!"

"Behind every fortune is a crime."

I'm crunching ice cubes from my Mandrin by the bar at the Malibu Pier View, scouring Jerry's novel for any sign of a salesman character. The book opens with this millionaire agent named Turk who blows himself up and leaves everything to his brother, but I've had too much to drink and I can't read anything anymore. I collect the pages together, straighten them on the bar counter, put the brick back in the box. Pretending to be sober, I sign for the bill, walk out of there, all skunk-like. I close my eyes and my world starts to spin—Not Good.

I open my eyes and now I'm exiting Colony House Liquors with two bags of crushed ice and four bottles of Mandrin. The Chrysler pulls into a scraping stop at a parking space at the Malibu Surfer Inn. I set down my plastic bags, buy a night at the Inn for $99.00 from the owner's bored, vaguely Asian daughter, who takes the receipt, snatches the pen out of my hand, and returns to her on-line conversation. Entering my room on the 3rd floor overlooking the water, I find an "aqua" motif of sea-green walls, school of fish shower curtain in the cramped bathroom quarters, and above the elaborately carved headboard: a flea market painting about the doomed voyage of the Essex ship stalked by an indefatigable white whale with harpoons sticking out of its casing.

Sliding open the balcony glass door, my nostrils inhale briny air, which has the effect of making me thirsty. I jam the quart of Mandrin into a bag of ice, twirl it around the cubes, prepare for my afternoon read. I take the Mandrin with Jerry's novel to the stone steps leading up to the elevated deck behind the motel. The sun-bleached roof of the Surfer Inn could use more tar. I pull up two filthy, once white plastic armchairs for me to sit. Across the PCH, the ocean glitter hypnotizes me until I remember what I came here to do. I try to focus on the words in Jerry's novel, but this breezy hillside view makes reading impossible, so I concentrate on the vodka. I shovel fistfuls of melting ice squares into a styrofoam cup, missing the rim, but for the most part filling it up. I take a gulp, chew the ice, start to read the manuscript when I think about my brother Jerry—

Outside the crowded garden area of the Silent Movie Theatre, I realized every woman here was topless, like a rule or something. Big-titted waitress offered me a drink from a hollowed-out longhorn—

"Watermelon shot?"

I opened my mouth to take a sickeningly sweet drink that splashed my tongue and cheek until I nodded to my server, enough.

"Road to Hell, Josh. Road to Hell," said my brother.

"What do you mean?"

"One day you will look back on your decision to enter the movie business with nothing but sadness and regret."

"That's you talking, bro. I know what I want."

"I'll make a few calls," he said.

"You're such a liar. I know you won't."

Socrates Wolinsky joined us along with his girlfriend, the bartender from the Mink Slide, her generous torso covered in black liquid latex.

"Let me guess, you're cold," I said.

"I can't feel anything. My tits are like frozen."

Siobhan said she wanted to be a "fucking actress," not "the other way around." I pointed to her matted posters of fuck films from CyberWhore.com.

"I got out last year. Syphilis is making a bigger comeback than me."

"Billboards are everywhere," I said.

"Sucks, doesn't it? Everybody's getting it."

"A simple case of the clap can turn into a whole round of applause."

I remember Jerry embarrassed me by regaling her with pathetic stories about my days as a bartender, tennis instructor, and hot dog cart salesman.

"What's your middle name?" Siobhan asked me, as if I mattered to her.

"David," I said.

"Name a street you raced on in high school."

"That I raced on? Battery Place."

"Your porn name is David Battery."

Socrates pulled his girlfriend away. Siobhan feigned being kidnapped—

"Don't forget to check out my farewell interactive DVD in the goody bag!"

Outside the Silent Movie Theatre, I was in a sour mood, out of my mind.

"Don't tell Socrates I tapped his girlfriend," said Jerry.

"When I move out here, stop putting me down."

"You're not moving out here," said Jerry.

"Why won't you help me?"

"I'm doing you a favor, bro."

"Stop acting like an only child."

"Have another drink," he laughed. "Fucking alkie."

I remember grabbing Jerry and throwing him against a dumpster in the bank parking lot. The last time I saw my brother alive, I kicked and punched him so many times he curled himself into a ball and never stopped screaming.

I'm loping around the house that Methuselah burnt, nervous as hell, waiting for Carmen when she finally shows up from the set of her new DQ movie. To the surprise of no one, Carmen got cast in Stanley's Cup opposite her co-star from the "aborted indie."

"I'm out of here," I say.

"Did you buy a loft downtown?"

"I'm leaving, Carmen. I should have listened to my brother. I'm putting the house up for sale."

"I don't get it."

"What part of I hate this stupid fucking business, hate the people, hate driving all the time, don't you understand?"

"If I bring you a beer, will you tell me what happened?"

"I don't drink. You may get me a seltzer."

Carmen sticks her head into the fridge, selects a Midas.

"Somebody's at the door," I say.

"That's Jessica. Call Electric Lotus. Remember she's vegan, so be considerate, Mr. Vindaloo. I need grin, got any?"

"Sorry, I don't have clients anymore. Lester buried Guru. The agency took him back."

Jessica appears, decked out in white.

"I like the leather cap, very Britney," says Carmen.

"Hey boss! What's the big secret?"

"I'm done with the business."

"Nobody just up and leaves the business," says Jessica.

"You think I'd be the first? Does this make me a pioneer?"

"If that's what you'd call this act of insanity. No one would believe you, anyway," says Jessica. "How's Dupin's new script?"

"How can you be talking about a script when I just told you I'm leaving?"

"Did you eat a bad piece of pizza at Damiano's?"

Jessica searches my eyes for a response when the phone rings somewhere in the Methuselah house. Jessica pulls Carmen into the media room to discuss my getaway plans. I grab the cordless. It's Dupin, and she sounds like she's about to heave herself off a ledge—

"Can I (sniff! sniff!) come over? I need (sniff! sniff!) to see you Guru!"

"What page are you on?"

"Don't! (sniff! sniff!) I can't even think about Turkey Legs! (sniff! sniff!) Script's done, all right? I just need to go through it once."

"Are you printing out as we speak?"

"Why are you being such a razor with me?"

"Because I can be. Bring it by later, okay? Jessica will read it."

"I want you to read it! I want the franchise! Promise me (sniff! sniff!) you won't leave until you've read my script."

"I'll call you from the road," I say.

In the media room: only a strobe-light flicker from the projection TV. I step closer to find Carmen splayed out on her elbows amidst a fort of pillows—

"You sure you want to leave, Josh?"

"Rubyfruit, wipe your chin," I say.

"Come here and lick it off," says Jessica, her face between parted legs.

Carmen arches her back and spreads herself open.

"People, can we all just get along?"

TURKEY LEGS

An Original Screenplay
by
Stefani Dupin

Registered WGAw

I liked the script so much I turned the Chrysler around in Flagstaff determined to make the studios pay dearly for it. Something in Dupin's script contaminated me, something I could weaponize, something everybody wants, and when you have something everybody wants in this business, it's worth staying an extra week. I knew I had gold after I read Dupin's terrific opening where the patriarch of the cop family chases and captures a fleeing bank robber and makes the perp apologize to the guy's wife on his cell for making him late to their anniversary. The grandfather was a hoot, more Jack Palance than Clint Eastwood, seeing criminals everywhere he went in public, foiling gunpoint muggings and rapes before they happened as if his dementia made him psychic. "Friday," the well-drawn and pivotal family hound, was a barking spinoff waiting to happen and a likely TV series if the movie should blow up the screens. I appreciated that Dupin had the cop family fighting themselves before, during, and after their battle with the menacing chain gang of escaped murderers. I really liked her font. I told Dupin she had the sister's cocaine part down. Then I paid her the highest compliment with two words a writer never hears in Hollywood: "No notes." It didn't help that Dupin fired her most recent agent, whose assistant passed on Turkey Legs, so I bought two full-page ads in the trades announcing the formation of Nobody. The ultimate outsiders, the surly party crashers, the unsolicited, that's us. We. Are. Nobody! Our focus was intense. We rented our own copier. I paid for Nobody script covers, Nobody business cards, and Nobody buck slips. We went out wide, hitting the 3 of Clubs, Jumbo's Clown Room, The Drawing Room, Jones, the Standard downtown, The Diaper Room, The Dresden, White Horse Inn, Lava, Swingers, Good Luck, outdoor patio at El Coyote, Mashti Malone's, The Spanish Kitchen, The Room, Zankou Chicken, Dragonfly, Pink's, Beauty Bar, The Magic Castle, Dominick's, Asanabo, Jones, Crazy Girls, Avalon, Skybar, Trader Vic's (which was totally fucking dead), Vida, Boardner's, Le Sex Shoppe, Hollywood Forever Cemetery, Formosa, Cheetahs, Dan Tana's, Hama Sushi, Cobras and Matadors, ABC Seafood in Chinatown, Jet Strip, Lola's, Katana, Brass Monkey, Star Shoes, Museum of Tolerance, the Velvet Margarita, Escape Room, Duke's, Pane e Vino, El Cholo (the one on Western), The Bounty, Ye Olde Rustic, 4100, Coach and Horses, until Jessica and I run into my Industry savior Orly Gold at the Shortstop, where I learn she has just published a successful How-To-Navigate-Your-Way-In-Hollywood guide. Orly blabs to Jessica about her beautiful wedding to her traffic school instructor, their awesome honeymoon in Wuhan, his refreshing lack of interest in all things Movie, and her itching to read a "family" script. I tell Orly I've got exactly what she's looking for. If there's one trick I learned from Lester Barnes (who's stopped taking my calls) it's to frown when you're with someone who just made you a millionaire. Put a frown on your true feelings. Let no one sense the exultation inside your heart now that a studio cashier has agreed to read Turkey Legs. In traffic school, Orly's husband must have blabbed to someone because Jessica told me Dimension has the script. Expect Warners to make an offer. I heard Bruce Berman is reading Turkey Legs on a plane with green eggs and ham.

"Are we alone on the line?" Brad Blumberg calls while

Jessica's at the Coffee Bean. "You and I are about to have a very unpleasant conversation."

"Piss on my parade, Esquire."

"Kate Hudson just told Disney she wants to do the picture with Kurt and Goldie but only if it's a family affair. I can probably get the studio to kiss you into the deal, after all, Dupin is your client, but Jessica's out."

"Their loss, it's a great script."

"You want a legal opinion? Lose the fresh cunt."

"Brad, I promised Jessica she could produce. You understand my sense of loyalty, right?"

"Quite frankly, I don't. Inviting your assistant into the deal for doing her job just isn't done. I told Psycho Killer she's out," he says.

"Psycho Killer?"

"Fa-Fa-Fa-Fa-Fa-Fa-Fa-Fa-Fa—that's what everybody at Omniscience called her after she said Jerry stole her pitch for Faith Don't Leave."

"Jessica wrote Faith Don't Leave?"

"Carrie Fisher didn't get credit for Pretty Woman, either. Lester blackballed Jessica after he expensed the abortion. I'll e-mail you the toilet paper."

No longer resembling the Fifth Bangle, a haggard-looking Dupin arrives at the Methusaleh house in uniform, gun holster slapping against her side, straight from a grueling 14-hour shift in Van Nuys, snorting coke right in front of me.

"I know who killed my brother," I announce.

"Tell me his name and I'll make the arrest right fucking now!"

"The assistant did it."

"Funny. Where is Jessica, anyway? She should be strategizing with us."

"Did you ever see Faith Don't Leave?"

"Oh my God I loved that movie, that movie was the best!"

"Jerry ripped off her idea for that movie. She was blackballed by Lester. She probably had a key to his office across the street—"

"Is this where you fuck Jessica out of the deal by blaming her for your brother's murder hours before the town starts making offers on the script you promised her she could produce? Damn, man, I thought I was hardcore."

"What kind of monster do you think I am?"

"You're my monster! Come here! I heard we're in at New Line!"

Dupin giddily smears her lips all over my mouth. I push away, repulsed.

"What's wrong? Don't I do it for you?"

"That was, unquestionably, the worst kiss of my life."

Dupin cracks me across the face—Slap! The hyphenate

cop turns away, stumbles slightly, makes a Z-axis towards the door.

I wake up in the blackness of the media room. I touch my throat to make sure it hasn't been slit. I see a figure cloaked in night descending the media room's circular stairwell and let loose a scream—

"I heard we're in at all the studios," says Jessica, one hand behind her back.

All my instincts they've returned.

"New Line passed. I brought you something."

I realize: life is real short.

"You wrote Faith Don't Leave."

"Who told you that, Lester? It was those lucky jerks who sold this action movie pitch to Beacon with Brad Pitt attached that, hello, still hasn't gotten made, and it is a testament to its utter mediocrity that it remains on a shelf!"

"Fa-Fa-Fa-Fa-Fa-Fa-Fa-Fa-Fa."

"You must have talked to Brad."

From downstairs, Dupin's voice: "Josh? (sniff! sniff!) Josh?"

"We're still alive at Paramount—"

Jessica raises her left arm to strike when the front of her face blows out in a corona of bone and maroon mist. A celebratory six-pack of Midas drops out of her hand. I push off Jessica, revealing Dupin with a smoking service revolver, who turns out to be the messiah and my reason to live.

I'm walking up a lonely wooded trail in Bronson Canyon with the vinyl bag holding Jerry's ashes. I knew I couldn't walk right up to the famous signage. I heard it had been fenced off to the public after an ingénue spent an afternoon auditioning for Darryl F. Zanuck and saw her future. I lift the plastic sack, break off the metal staple, and release his cremains below the nine white letters when my cell vibrates, caller ID: UNKNOWN. An assistant announces Dave LaVache at Fox Business Affairs calling from his car—

"Who the fuck gave you this number?"

"How are you today, sir?"

"I didn't know I had been knighted," I say.

Another BLOCKED NUMBER calls.

"I'm kind of busy right now. Can I call you back, Dave?"

"Remind me, what was the writer's last quote?"

"Hold on for just one second, one second, will you? Let me get rid of this other caller."

Click. I hear a man breathing heavily into the receiver as if he had just run up the Empire State building.

"I know you're excited, but can you catch your breath before you make me an offer?"

"You're asking too much for it." asks Breathless. "I'll give you three for it, there's another one on the market."

"With bonus, what are you talking about?"

"Didn't say nothing about a bonus—"

"Hold on, okay? I got a buyer on the other line," I say.

Click over to La Vache.

"Dave, I was just offered three!"

"Bullshit. If I find out you're lying to me—"

"I have a guy on the other line offering three hundred."

"Tell whoever is holding I hope they get Cancer."

I click over to Breathless.

"What studio are you calling from?"

"I'm calling about the Saab on Craig's List," he says.

"No offense, but the guy on the other line can spank your offer."

"I had my eye on a Camaro anyway."

Click over to LaVache from Fox.

"Our offer's three against six. Take it or hang up," says LaVache.

On my phone, caller ID: BLOCKED NUMBER.

"See you in the next life."

Click. It's Lou Knockalara, business affairs, for U.

"I just turned down two offers, Lou—Not Good."

"We're not overpaying for this script, she's not getting her quote. I'll tell you what she's getting: how about we give her a blind script deal on top of the purchase, mutually agreed upon, it can be a pitch, an open writing assignment, or a production polish with a director, maybe she wants to adapt something."

"Save your breath for the blowup doll in your wife's closet."

"Offer expires at noon, you putz."

"I didn't hear an offer."

I hang up. Take the call from Neufchatel, at Sony.

"We're taking it off your hands, right now, on this call: 450 for the script, guaranteed rewrites, production bonus takes you to $900,000."

Another incoming. I ignore it.

"I just got off the horn with Nikolovski at Omniscience," I say.

"How's my brother-in-law doing?"

"He told me you have the IQ of a Krispy Kreme."

"I'm crowning," says Neufchatel.

"Which dwarf are you, again? Just kidding, I'm calling the writer now."

Click over to: Gwartz from Paramount.

"We want to make a statement. One million, 500 bonus. If you have to call me back, the offer is withdrawn, and I will perjure myself denying I ever said anything to you."

Caller ID: DUPIN.

"That's the writer calling. I am going to tell her I support Paramount's offer."

I click over to a beyond-excited Dupin.

"Make them pay, guru!"

"Did you give notice yet?"

"Now that your brother's case is closed, you bet."

"I think I can get a little more out of Paramount."

"Take the offer. We're back in the sandbox. Close the deal. What do you want?"

"I want them to buy me a bar."

"Do you know which one?"

"I know exactly the bar I want," I say.

"Then you go right ahead and tell Paramount to buy you the bar. If they say no, try Regency. Make the call, Josh, close the fucking deal."

I wanted to repair my friendship with Socrates so I invited the editor to Franklin's memorial service at some French actor's house in Whitley Heights. His walking-talking Daily Variety desperation became hard to take after I told him I had gotten his script over to Matthew McConaughey through someone who knew someone who'd had lunch with someone who knew the roommate of someone who worked at Crunch. The speeches in Whitley Heights were similar to the outrage usually expressed at a victim's rally. Franklin didn't pull the trigger. It was the Industry. I wondered who all these people were and where were they during the last year and a half of Franklin's life when two projects in a row collapsed?

"McConaughey's agent called me today."

"Called you back or did you speak to him?"

"Socrates, I am the loop. Don't look so suspicious."

"So, where and when's the meeting?"

"First you do McConaughey's agent's assistant's notes, then all I have to do is get Screen Gems to come in for half, then—"

"Forget it, Josh. McConaughey's not right for the part anyway. Do you like filet mignon?"

"I love filet mignon."

"With béarnaise sauce. What about lobster tails?"

"Surf and turf! Where is it, Socrates? Over by that table where what's his name is standing with his whore?"

"What if I told you I could get you, delivered to your door in about a week, two filet mignons, two lobster tails, the vegetable of your choice, and two chocolate desserts?"

"That's awesome. Thanks, Socrates."

"I just need your credit card number."

"You're a meat pusher?"

"Last week? I went to Studio City and sold a box of beef tenderloin for Corbin Bernson!"

"Sign me up, Socrates. Can we do this later?"

"Let's do the credit card number now."

I reach for my cell and start to dial 911—

LOS ANGELES TIMES

LAPD HAS "FAITH" AGENT'S KILLER

HOLLYWOOD—With no leads, a long list of suspects, and a false confession, the unsolved murder of Hollywood agent Jerry Makos had all the makings of the popular CBS show, "Cold Case."

Socrates Wolinsky, 33, a part-time meat vendor and film editor was arrested yesterday and charged with first degree murder, which could bring him the death penalty.

"With justice, we have peace," said DQ in a statement from an undisclosed substance abuse center where he is undergoing treatment.

Omniscience's Lester Barnes, unaware that California executions are by lethal injection, said, "Let him dangle."

Calls to Josh Makos were not returned.

I'm checking inventory behind the counter of the bar formerly known as the Mink Slide when a gaunt gentleman in a metallic gray Prada suit walks in—

"That's a very unique cigar store Indian you've got over there."

"Thanks. I won it in Park City."

"What do you have on tap?"

"Bass, Hefenweisen, Sierra Nevada, Guinness, Sam Adams."

"What do you have in the bottle, domestic?"

"Bud, Bud Light, Heineken, but that's not domestic, sorry, Miller Genuine Draft, Miller Light, Michelob—"

"Michelob! That's what I'll have!"

"Who's your trainer, Lester? Dr. 90210?"

"I was with Nikolovski the other day, two of us putting our heads together over at Omniscience, we thought you might want to make your business life more interesting. How does a hundred grand a year as a lit agent grab you?"

"I'm out of the Industry, Lester."

"What Industry?"

"I read Jerry's novel. Any of it true?"

"He shouldn't have written about staff meetings. You don't talk about what goes on in my house. What happens inside my house stays in my house!"

"What about Jerry and your wife and that disgusting bukkake movie they shot on your tennis court?"

"They shot a bukkake? Where the hell was I?"

"You and Nikolovski knew what was going on with IFD and Jerry's side deals with Benny Pantera. You should've watched out for him—"

"Hey, I protected him, he saw some money—"

"You don't understand! He was my brother, Lester! You should've taken care of him, you should've taken care of him just a little bit at year-end, so he wouldn't have had only enemies for friends!"

"Let me tell you something about your clotheshorse brother who fucked summer interns in his office and chased pussy like a parked car—"

"That's it, you're 86'd!"

Lester's untouched Michelob: sweeped off the bar, thrown into a bin.

"This monkey at the Zoo sneaks into the Lion Exhibit and starts fucking the lion in the ass. Lion realizes what's happening, freaks, and chases the monkey. Monkey turns a corner, snags a seat on a bench, dons a pair of shades and a hat, and pretends to be reading Variety. Lion comes racing around the corner, furious, sees the monkey in disguise, asks him if he just saw a monkey. Monkey looks up from his Variety and says, 'You mean the monkey who fucked the lion in the ass?' And the lion says, 'What! It's in the trades already?'"

"You're infected with the business."

"I know, we all are, isn't the virus great?"

HITCHED

Ruth Furfari and Ezra Haneke, July 25, San Francisco. Bride is subtitle and closed-captioning administrator for the international department at Telemundo. Groom's maternal grandmother is the caterer.

Amber Ridder and Benjamin Nabul, August 1, New York City. Bride's a freelance unit publicist; groom's director of affiliate sales, Western region, at the Weather Channel.

Carmen Coronado and Josh Makos, August 8, San Diego. Bride's the Actress; groom's non-pro.

CALL SHEET

Doonesbury
Stephen King
R.M. Koster
John O'Brien
Donald Cammell
The Morris Office
KG, JML, JCG, DG, AJ, WM, JS, BMS, JY, HM, JA, AH, VM, LW, CM, LK, BJM, AC, KOR, ERE, WHITT
Lauren
JD
The Rabbi
Max
Jason
Sara
Laurie
Patti
Mark
Roger
Marvin
Sykes
Damian
Gwen
Sag
Mormor
Barbara Novak
Brian O'Doherty
Jonathan
Mom and Dad
Zonker